"When I close my eyes, I see your face."

His words, so gravel-rough, had her heart racing.

"You're driving me crazy. Taking over every moment of my life."

She couldn't breathe. Because what he was saying—that was the way she felt. As if he'd taken over her life.

"I tried to walk away. I tried to be strong." He lowered his head.

"Gunner..."

"There are some lines that if you cross them, you can't ever go back."

"I don't want to go back." There was nothing in her past to go back to.

"I won't be able to let you go."

She wouldn't let him go. Before Gunner could say anything else, Sydney wrapped her hands around his neck and pulled his head down toward her.

D0324435

Dear Harlequin Intrigue Reader,

For nearly thirty years fearless romance has fueled every Harlequin Intrigue book. Now we want everyone to know about the great crime stories our fantastic authors write and the variety of compelling miniseries we offer. We think our new cover look complements and enhances our promise to deliver edge-of-your-seat reads in all six of our titles—and brand-new titles every month!

This month's lineup is packed with nonstop mystery in *Smoky Ridge Curse,* the third in Paula Graves's Bitterwood P.D. trilogy, exciting action in *Sharpshooter,* the next installment in Cynthia Eden's Shadow Agents miniseries, and of course fearless romance—whether from newcomers Jana DeLeon and HelenKay Dimon or veteran author Aimée Thurlo, we've got every angle covered.

Next month buckle up as Debra Webb returns with a new Colby Agency series featuring The Specialists. And in November *USA TODAY* bestselling author B.J. Daniels takes us back to "The Canyon" for her special *Christmas at Cardwell Ranch* celebration.

Lots going on and lots more to come. Be sure to check out www.Harlequin.com for what's coming next.

Enjoy,

Denise Zaza

Senior Editor

Harlequin Intrigue

SHARPSHOOTER

USA TODAY Bestselling Author
CYNTHIA EDEN

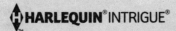

If you purchased this book without a cover you should be aware
that this book is stolen property. It was reported as "unsold and
destroyed" to the publisher, and neither the author nor the
publisher has received any payment for this "stripped book."

Recycling programs
for this product may
not exist in your area.

I wanted to offer a huge thank-you to all the
wonderful folks at Harlequin Intrigue. It is always
a pleasure! And for my friend Joan, a woman who
loves her strong heroes, I hope you enjoy this story.

ISBN-13: 978-0-373-69704-5

SHARPSHOOTER

Copyright © 2013 by Cindy Roussos

All rights reserved. Except for use in any review, the reproduction or
utilization of this work in whole or in part in any form by any electronic,
mechanical or other means, now known or hereafter invented, including
xerography, photocopying and recording, or in any information storage
or retrieval system, is forbidden without the written permission of the
publisher, Harlequin Enterprises Limited, 225 Duncan Mill Road,
Don Mills, Ontario M3B 3K9, Canada.

This is a work of fiction. Names, characters, places and incidents are
either the product of the author's imagination or are used fictitiously,
and any resemblance to actual persons, living or dead, business
establishments, events or locales is entirely coincidental.

This edition published by arrangement with Harlequin Books S.A.

For questions and comments about the quality of this book,
please contact us at CustomerService@Harlequin.com.

® and TM are trademarks of Harlequin Enterprises Limited or its
corporate affiliates. Trademarks indicated with ® are registered in the
United States Patent and Trademark Office, the Canadian Trade Marks
Office and in other countries.

Printed in U.S.A.

ABOUT THE AUTHOR

USA TODAY bestselling author Cynthia Eden writes tales of romantic suspense and paranormal romance. Her books have received starred reviews from *Publishers Weekly,* and she has received a RITA® Award nomination for best romantic suspense novel. Cynthia lives in the deep South, loves horror movies and has an addiction to chocolate. More information about Cynthia may be found on her website, www.cynthiaeden.com, or you can follow her on Twitter (www.twitter.com/cynthiaeden).

Books by Cynthia Eden

HARLEQUIN INTRIGUE
1398—ALPHA ONE*
1404—GUARDIAN RANGER*
1437—SHARPSHOOTER*

*Shadow Agents

All backlist available in ebook. Don't miss any of our special offers. Write to us at the following address for information on our newest releases.

Harlequin Reader Service
U.S.: 3010 Walden Ave., P.O. Box 1325, Buffalo, NY 14269
Canadian: P.O. Box 609, Fort Erie, Ont. L2A 5X3

CAST OF CHARACTERS

Gunner Ortez—Gunner has never been able to control his feelings for Sydney Sloan, the woman who was once engaged to his brother. But now that he has a chance to finally make Syndey his, Gunner isn't going to let anyone or anything stand in his way.

Sydney Sloan—Sydney can tell when she is in the sights of a killer. But she isn't sure who she should trust. Putting her faith in the wrong man may just lead to her death.

Slade Ortez—He should have been a dead man, but when Slade is discovered—very much alive—in Peru, his appearance rips right through the new life that Gunner and Sydney are building. Slade's appearance also sets off an explosive chain of events that will rock right through the Elite Operations Division.

Cale Lane—The former army ranger is determined to protect his teammates, but sometimes even a trained hunter can't see the danger coming until it is far too late.

Logan Quinn—The team leader of the EOD, Logan is intimately acquainted with the risks associated with his job. But when it looks as if a member of his team is actually turning on the EOD, Logan knows that he could be in for the most dangerous battle of his life.

Prologue

The thunder of gunfire erupted around her as Sydney Sloan ran through the remains of the enemy's camp. Voices were calling out, screaming, but she didn't stop. She couldn't.

Her focus was on the man before her. The man lying so still in the middle of that nightmare scene.

"Slade!" Her own scream joined the others as she fell to her knees beside him. She grabbed for his shoulder and rolled him toward her.

His chest was a bloody mess. His eyes—those dark eyes that she'd stared into so many times—were closed. "Slade?" she whispered hoarsely. No, this couldn't happen. They were supposed to get out of there together. They were going to start their life together back in the States. They were going to get married.

"I'll get you out of here." He *would* be fine. She'd get him to the helicopter. Fly him out of there. He'd get patched up, and everything would be just as they'd planned.

More gunfire erupted. Her breath choked out when a bullet drove into her shoulder. The pain burned her, terrified her. If she was hurt too badly, how would she get Slade to safety?

She grabbed his arms. Started to drag him.

More gunfire. This time, the bullet hit her in the side. She stumbled but refused to fall. Slade needed her. She wasn't going to let him down.

"Sydney!" The roar of her name had her jerking up her head. She saw Gunner Ortez then, running toward her and his brother.

Gunner and Slade. They were so different. Slade was always laughing, so easygoing. Gunner was intense, almost… frightening to her.

But she knew Gunner would do anything for his brother. "Help him!" Sydney called as her knees buckled. She hit the ground, still holding tight to Slade.

Why weren't her knees working? Why did she feel so cold? It was so hot in the jungle.

Then Gunner was there. He was curling his body around hers, shielding her from the hail of gunfire that just wouldn't stop.

A trap. They'd walked right into this hell because they'd been going after Slade. A rescue mission. They'd had to take the risk of infiltrating the area, against orders.

Gunner's fingers—long, tan, strong—went to Slade's throat. She felt the thick tension in the big body behind hers as Gunner checked for his brother's pulse. Then Gunner swore.

No. *No.*

His hand pulled back. She grabbed his fingers. Held tight. "You have to help me," she whispered. "Gunner, please, we have to get him out of here!"

More gunfire. Gunner curled his body even tighter to hers. She heard the thud of the impact and knew he'd just taken a bullet.

For her.

"He's not here anymore," Gunner rasped. His eyes—as dark as Slade's but lined with gold flecks, stared into her own. *"He's not here."*

She shook her head.

The *rat-a-tat* of gunfire came again. Gunner yanked out a handgun with his left hand. He began to fire back, even as the fingers of his right hand twisted and locked with hers. "We have to get out of here! We're damn sitting ducks!"

"Not without…Slade…" Her side *hurt*. A deep, agonizing burn, and she wondered just how bad the hit was. But she'd make it, she'd hold on, until they got Slade out of there. They'd come to rescue him, and they'd never failed on a mission before. *"Help me."*

The gold in his eyes seemed to blaze. "How many times have you been hit?"

Two? Three? What did it matter? "Slade…"

Then she heard the roar of engines. Coming toward them. The enemy closing in. There wasn't any more time. "Just… *take him.*" Because she wasn't sure that she'd be able to get out on her own steam. She couldn't make her legs work, and as she pulled her fingers from Gunner's, she realized that she was shaking. She'd run out of ammo, and the blood was pumping down her side. "Take him…please." Her voice broke and her body began to sway. She was already on her knees, but Sydney was pretty sure she'd soon slump forward and crash face-first into the dirt.

Hold it together. Stay strong, just until Slade is safe.

But Gunner's hands didn't wrap around Slade's body. His hands reached for her.

She screamed then, and lunged toward Slade.

But Gunner pulled her back. The bullets were hitting the ground around her, sending chunks of dirt flying into the air. They had no cover, no backup and it sounded as though more enemy reinforcements were coming in.

Shouldn't have been here. Shouldn't have happened. How had everything gotten so messed up? Their cover had been blown pretty much from the get-go.

"Gunner, no." She tried to pull away from him. "Can't… leave…"

Another bullet hit her. Driving through her upper shoulder and sinking into Gunner.

She choked, barely managing to breathe as the pain swamped her.

"He's dead," Gunner gritted out. She was in his arms then. He was holding her tight, bruising her. "You…*won't* be."

Sydney fought him, using all the strength that she had, but she didn't have enough. Gunner was wounded, too, but nothing stopped him. Not ever.

So he ran right through the gunfire, holding her in arms like steel. He ran and ran, and then they were in the heavier, denser part of the jungle, evading the men who chased them. No jeeps could follow them here.

Gunner wouldn't let her go, no matter how much she begged him.

He didn't speak to her again. Didn't say a word.

And behind them, in that nightmare, Slade remained in the dirt.

Dead.

His eyes had never opened. From the time she'd fallen by his side, he hadn't moved. Hadn't spoken. Hadn't even been able to open his eyes.

They never would open again.

GUNNER GOT HER out of that jungle. Patched her up. Stopped the blood flow. She wasn't helping him. Sydney was barely moving at all.

"Shock," Gunner told her, voice terse.

Yeah, that was it. She had to be in shock. Because she'd just seen her fiancé die in that trap. She and Slade had fought before, and for him to die with that anger between them...*I'm so sorry.*

"You lost too much blood." Gunner's fingers curled around her chin. She didn't know where they were now. Some kind of hut? A run-down shack? Just some shelter he'd found them. Gunner was good at finding shelters. "You *won't* die."

Hadn't he said that before? It was hard to remember. Her tongue seemed so thick in her mouth, but after three tries she managed to say, "Slade..."

Gunner's fingers tightened on her. "He's gone."

A tear leaked down her cheek.

Gunner's jaw clenched. That hard jaw. That dangerous face. "I've got you, Syd. I'll take care of you."

She was breaking apart on the inside. The mission was over. They'd failed.

He pulled her into his arms. Held her against his chest. Gentleness? He'd never seemed the kind for that. "I've got you," he said again, voice deepening.

And it was there, in his arms, that she finally let herself go.

She cried until there were no tears left to shed.

Chapter One

Two years later...

Two years later...

The kidnapper had a gun pressed to Sydney's head.

Gunner Ortez stopped breathing when he saw Sydney's beautiful face fill his scope. So perfect. Delicate, high cheekbones. The soft curve of her nose. The full, red lips...

And the green eyes that stared straight back at him. Seeming to *know* where he was. Her green gaze that showed no fear even as that soon-to-be-dead man jammed the gun harder into her temple.

"Do you have the shot?" a low voice asked in his ear. The earpiece wouldn't even be noticed by most people. Uncle Sam was great at inventing gear that his soldiers could use anytime, anyplace.

With a minimum of fuss and a maximum of damage.

Gunner's finger was curled over the trigger, but he wasn't taking the shot. "Negative, Alpha One," he told his team leader. "Sydney isn't clear."

And he was sweating, feeling a tendril of fear—when he *never* felt fear. There was no room for emotion on any of their missions.

He worked with a group far off the grid. The Elite Ops Division wasn't on any books anywhere in the U.S. government. They took the jobs that the rest of the world wasn't meant to know about. In particular, his EOD team—code-named the Shadow Agents—had a reputation for deadly accuracy when it came to taking out their targets.

And this guy…that jerk with the trembling finger, he was going down. The man had kidnapped an ambassador's daughter. Held her for ransom, and when the ransom had been paid, he'd still killed her.

He'd thought he could hide from justice.

He'd thought wrong.

Sydney's intel had led them to Jonathan Hall. Led them to his hideout just over the border in Mexico.

Sydney had volunteered to go in, to make sure that Hall was holding no civilians.

Now she was the one being held.

"He can't leave the scene," Logan Quinn said, the faint drawl of the South sliding beneath the team leader's words as they carried easily over the transmitter. "You know our orders."

Containment or death. Yeah, Gunner knew the drill, because the ambassador's daughter hadn't been the first victim. Hall liked to kill.

Gunner stared down at the man, at Sydney. *You won't kill her.*

Sydney's face was emotionless. Like a pale canvas, waiting for life. That wasn't her. She was always brimming with emotion, letting it spill over onto everything and everyone.

It was only on the missions that she changed.

How many more missions would she take? She seemed to be putting herself at risk more these days. He *hated* that.

He shifted his position, testing the wind. Hall wouldn't see him. He was too far away. Gunner's specialty was attacking from a distance.

There was no target that he couldn't reach.

He could take out that man right now. A perfect shot…

if he hadn't been worried that Hall's finger would jerk on that trigger at impact.

"I want the gun away from her head," Gunner snapped into his mouthpiece.

But even as he said the words, he saw Sydney's lips moving.

Take. The. Shot.

Hall was outside the small house, his gaze frantically searching the area even as he kept Sydney killing-close. The man wasn't stupid. He'd eluded capture for over a year because he understood how the game was played.

Hall knew Sydney hadn't come in alone. The guy just didn't see her backup. When he hunted like this, Gunner's prey never saw him, not unless he wanted to be seen.

This time, he wanted to be seen because that gun *was* coming away from Sydney's head.

Take. The. Shot. Her lips moved again.

He shook his head, even though he realized she'd never see the movement. Then he took two steps to the right. He knew that, in this particular position, the sunlight would glint off his weapon. When he saw that flash of light, Hall would fire—

And he did. The man yanked the gun away from Sydney's head and shot at Gunner.

Too late.

Gunner had already taken his own shot.

The second the gun moved away from her temple, Sydney shoved back against Hall with her elbow, and then she'd jerked away from her captor and threw herself down.

Before she even hit the ground, Gunner's bullet slammed into Hall. The man stumbled back and fell.

"Converge," Logan's hard order came in Gunner's ear.

The other EOD team members rushed from the shadows. Not that they needed to rush. Hall wasn't going to be a threat to anyone, not anymore.

Gunner's breath eased out. He watched as Sydney pushed to her knees, then rose to her feet.

Cale Lane, the newest team member, crouched over Hall as Sydney looked toward Gunner's position.

He'd put the weapon down, so he couldn't see her face clearly, not with the distance that separated them. But he was aware that his heart beat too fast. His hands had been sweating.

A sharpshooter wasn't supposed to get nervous, wasn't supposed to *feel* on the mission.

But whenever he was close to Sydney, all he could do was feel.

He packed up his weapon and hurried down to her. Because lately, it was always about her.

Day and night. Whether he was awake or asleep, he was obsessed with the woman.

Cale and Logan had secured the scene by the time he got down to the front of the house, and Cale was leading some sobbing redhead from the cabin. So Sydney had been right. Hall had already taken his next victim. If they hadn't moved then, would she have been dead by nightfall?

"Good shot." Sydney's voice was quiet.

Gunner's body tensed. He knew he should hold on to his control, but…*the gun had been at her temple.* If Hall hadn't hesitated, Gunner would have watched while the man put a hole in her head.

So he ignored the wide stare that Logan gave him and stalked to Sydney. He grabbed her wrist, pulled her against him. "You took too much of a risk."

Her short blond hair shone in the light. Her cheeks stained red—he didn't know if that red was from fury or embarrassment.

"I did my job," Sydney said through gritted teeth, lifting her chin. "I told you that my intel indicated a new hostage. She was hidden in the closet. If I hadn't moved in—"

He pulled her even closer. "He could have killed you."

Then what would I have done?

Her voice dropped. "You say it like that matters to you." Her words were whispered, carrying only to his ears.

Damn it, she did matter. "Sydney..."

"You're the one who wants to be hands-off," she snapped with a hard flash of her green eyes. "So why are you holding on to me so tightly?"

He was. Too tightly. He dropped her wrist as if he'd been burned.

"I'm not waiting any longer," Sydney told him as she straightened her shoulders. "Death can come at any moment, and I told you once...I'm not crawling into the grave with Slade."

Yes, she'd told him that, when he'd made the mistake of getting too close to Sydney on their last case. They'd been trapped during a storm, forced together in a small cabin, and all he'd been able to think was...

I want her.

But he'd—*barely*—managed to stop himself from taking what he wanted. He did have some self-control. Unfortunately, with her, that self-control was growing weaker every day.

"I'm going to start living my life on *my* terms," Sydney told him. "Consider yourself warned."

Then she spun away. Sydney headed toward Cale and the redhead. More backup had swarmed the scene. Other EOD agents who'd come to lend their support for the rescue-and-takedown operation.

Gunner stared after Sydney, feeling...lost.

Then Logan cleared his throat. "I've seen that look before."

Gunner glared at him. Logan might be the team leader for the Shadow Agents, and Gunner considered him as a friend most days, but the man should know not to—

"Better watch yourself, or you might just lose something important."

Sydney had already walked away. Logan didn't understand.

She was never mine to lose.

THE BAR WAS too loud. The place was packed with too many people, and coming there, well, it had been a serious mistake.

Sydney huffed out a hard breath and pushed her barely sipped drink away. She'd gotten back to the States just hours before—finally gotten a break for some serious R & R time, and she'd gone home to Baton Rouge.

But it didn't feel like home anymore.

So many missions. So many places.

They were all blending together into a hail of gunfire and death.

"A pretty lady like you shouldn't be sitting alone." The voice, marked with the Cajun that she loved, came from her right.

Sydney's gaze rose, and she found herself staring at a tall, blond man. He was handsome, with the kind of good looks that probably drew women all the time.

So why isn't he drawing me?

She'd come to that bar to find someone like him. It seemed as if she'd been living in a void for the past two years of her life, and she wanted—so desperately wanted— to start feeling again.

The blond glanced at her drink. "Don't you like it?"

Sydney shook her head. "It's not what I wanted."

He pulled up the bar stool next to her, leaned in close. "Why don't you tell me what you want?"

A stranger, a guy who didn't know her at all, and he looked at her with more warmth than Gunner did.

Don't think about him. This was not supposed to be another Gunner night.

She forced a smile on her face. Gunner was miles away. He always had been. This man, he was right in front of her. She wanted to live, and here was her chance. "I'm really not sure," she said softly. The words were the truth.

What did she want?

Gunner.

That wasn't happening. Time to consider other options.

The guy leaned toward her. "How about we start with a dance, then? Maybe that will help you figure out just what you want."

How long had it been since she'd danced with someone? Too long.

"I'm Colin," he said, giving her a broad smile. "And I promise, I'm a good guy."

As if she could believe a promise from a stranger. She'd met far too many dangerous, lying men for that.

"I'm Sydney." She took the hand that he offered to her. "I guess one dance—"

She broke off, her words stuttering to a halt because she'd just met the dark gaze of the man who'd entered the bar. A man who should *not* have been there.

A man whose stare was hot enough to burn.

Colin stiffened beside her as he followed her gaze. "Problem?"

Yes. No. Maybe. If Gunner was there, then there could be a new mission. There *had* to be a new mission. There was no other reason for Gunner to be in Baton Rouge instead of up in D.C.

But why hadn't Logan just called her?

Gunner was stalking toward her.

"I thought you were here alone," Colin said softly.

"I am." He still had her hand, and that felt wrong all of a sudden.

Maybe because Gunner's gaze had dipped to their hands. Hardened.

"Then you want to tell me why that guy looks like he's about to rip me apart?"

Gunner did look that way. But Gunner *usually* looked tough. It was his face. Not handsome like Colin's. Not perfect. It was full of hard angles and dangerous edges. With his golden skin and that jet-black hair, he always looked like walking, talking danger to Sydney.

Danger wasn't supposed to draw you in, but Gunner seemed to draw her more and more.

Even as he kept pushing her away.

"He's a friend," Sydney said, giving a shrug that she hoped looked careless. "An old friend."

Then Gunner was in front of them. "Sydney." His voice was a deep, rumbling growl when Colin's voice had been soft and flirtatious. Did Gunner even know how to flirt? She doubted it. "We need to talk."

A mission. Right. Just as she'd suspected. Sydney cleared her throat and glanced at Colin. His hold was light on her wrist. "Can you give us just a minute?"

One blond eyebrow rose, but he nodded. "I'll wait for you." She noticed that when he glanced back at Gunner, Colin's face hardened, losing some of its easygoing appeal.

Gunner didn't wait for the guy to back away. He grabbed Sydney's hand—his grip much tighter than Colin's—and pulled her into the nearest dark corner.

"Gunner!" His name burst from her. "What are you doing?"

He caged her with his body. "What are *you* doing?"

"Getting a drink? Getting ready to dance?" Some things should be obvious to a superagent like him.

His teeth snapped together as he leaned in, even closer. The wooden wall was behind her, and Gunner's muscled form wasn't leaving much space in front of her. "You know what he wants."

She was in some kind of weird alternate reality. Sydney shook her head. "What's the mission? Why didn't Logan call—"

"There is no mission."

She didn't have any kind of comeback. She couldn't think of what to say. If there was no mission, then Gunner shouldn't be in Louisiana. Her family's old home was there, but Gunner had a place in D.C. Not here.

"I could see it in your eyes," he growled.

"See what?" Her voice came out huskier than she'd intended.

Gunner flinched. "After the last mission, I knew you'd do something like this." He glanced over his shoulder. Since Gunner was big, easily six foot three, with wide shoulders, she couldn't see what he was looking at when he glared behind him.

But she had a pretty good idea.

Colin.

"Any man?" Gunner asked as that hard, dark gaze came back to her. "Is that what you're—"

Her cheeks felt numb. "Don't say another word." She wanted to slug him. "You don't have the right to say anything to me, to judge me." She'd wanted Gunner, had let him become too important to her in the past few years, but *enough.* "Slade is gone. I've moved on." She pushed at him.

Gunner stepped back.

Good. She marched away from him and didn't look back.

Colin stood as she approached. "I want that dance," Sydney said, and she pretty much dragged him onto the small floor.

She didn't know what Gunner's game was. But he wasn't controlling her. He didn't want her. He'd made that clear when she'd tried to kiss him on that case in Texas.

Colin's hands settled along her hips. She was wearing a pair of jeans, a top that was a little low and strappy sandals that pushed her a bit higher than her normal five-foot-six height. Colin was big, not as tall or muscled as Gunner, and—

"You don't want to come between us."

Gunner was *there*. Again. On the dance floor. And he'd just pulled Colin away from her.

This was insane.

"Sydney, come with me," Gunner said in that low growl of his.

Colin shook his head. "Look, buddy, I don't care if you are her friend, you don't—"

"Is that what I am, Sydney?" Gunner asked, his voice flat. "Your friend?

He had been. After that nightmare two years ago, he'd become her rock. The man she depended on. The one who'd pulled her through her darkest time.

But she wanted him to be more than that.

She wanted *more*.

He didn't.

"I don't know what you are," she told him. "But you should leave." Because she was tired of living only for the job. She'd find happiness. Everyone else did. She wanted to have a real home one day. A family.

Not just mission after mission.

Why couldn't someone be waiting on her when she came home? Someone who loved her? Wanted her?

"You heard the lady," Colin muttered.

But Gunner wasn't moving. He *had* started to give Colin a killing glare.

Colin made the mistake of stepping toward Gunner. Of shoving against his chest. "You need to *back off*—" Colin began.

Definitely a mistake.

Gunner grabbed that shoving hand and twisted it. Colin's words choked off, and the dancers around them froze as they realized what was happening.

In less than three seconds, Gunner had Colin on his knees…all from that hold that Gunner had on Colin's hand. Sydney knew the twist that Gunner was using could be incredibly painful, and if Gunner just pulled a little more, Colin's bones would snap.

This scene was turning into a nightmare.

"Gunner, let him go!" Sydney grabbed his arm. "You're making a scene!"

"No, *he* did that when he shoved me." But Gunner let the other man go.

Colin scrambled away, eyes wide, cheeks flushed. He headed for the door as fast as he could.

Well, so much for that dance. So much for the whole night. Sydney turned from Gunner and started marching for the door. The plan had been stupid, anyway. As if she was going to find some kind of Prince Charming in a bar like this.

She pushed open the front door, and the night air rushed over her. Sydney took two more steps, then…

She stopped. "Tell me that you aren't following me home." Because she *knew* he was behind her. As a rule, Gunner could move pretty soundlessly. That was one of the reasons he'd been so good during his time as a SEAL sharpshooter. But she could *feel* him, so she knew he was trailing her.

"We need to talk."

Fabulous. "I thought there wasn't anything to say. I mean, you had your chance at Whiskey Ridge…" When she'd ditched her pride and told him that she needed him.

But he'd stayed aloof.

Gunner always held back with her. Always saw the ghost of her fiancé, *his half brother,* between them.

She knew now that he wasn't ever going to let that ghost go. She might want Gunner. Want him so badly that her heart had seemed to break when he kept pulling away, but she'd survive his rejection.

She'd survived much worse than not being wanted by Gunner Ortez.

"What do you want from me?" Gunner asked her.

Everything.

Sydney turned toward him. "I want you to look at me and just see a woman. Not a ghost."

A muscle jerked in his jaw. "You're pushing me too much."

She shook her head. "I'm not pushing you at all. You're the one who came here, to *my town.* You're the one who showed up in the bar." Frustrated, she demanded, "How did you even find me here? Did you follow my GPS location?" All of the EOD agents had trackers installed on their phones. But if he'd used that tracking system… *Stalker much.* "Now I'm the one walking away."

Only she didn't get to walk far. Four steps was all she took. Then Gunner's hands were on her shoulders. He spun her back around and lifted her up on her tiptoes.

"When I close my eyes, I see your face."

His words, so gravel-rough, had her heart racing.

"I don't see a ghost, I just see you." His eyes were on her mouth. "You're driving me crazy, taking over every moment of my life."

She couldn't breathe. Because what he was saying—that was the way she felt. As if he'd taken over her life.

"I tried to walk away. I tried to be strong." His head lowered. "But I don't want you to be with anyone else."

Sydney didn't want to be with any other man. "Gunner…"

"There are some lines that if you cross them, you can't ever go back."

"I don't want to go back." There was nothing in her past to go back to. Only death.

Gunner was life.

"I won't be able to let you go."

She wouldn't let him go. Before Gunner could say anything else, Sydney wrapped her hands around his neck and she pulled his head down toward her.

The kiss wasn't easy or gentle. Wasn't the tentative kiss of soon-to-be lovers.

It was hard and deep—consuming. The touch of his lips sent need spiraling through her. Then she was crushed against him. Holding on as tight as she could as he tasted her, and she tasted him, and all of the longing that she'd held inside so tightly broke from her control.

This was Gunner. This wasn't a dream. This was real.

And there was no going back.

HE SHOULD LET her go. Gunner knew he shouldn't have followed her to Baton Rouge, but he'd been afraid.

I don't want to lose her.

Sydney Sloan. The woman he'd wanted since the moment he first met her. Even when she'd been planning to marry his brother, Gunner had wanted her.

They were back at her house. He'd followed her from the bar, feeling the hunger for her burn just beneath his skin.

She stood on the porch now. The swamp waited behind her, and the sound of crickets filled the air.

He was closing in on her. There was still time to pull back, still time to do the right thing.

But he wasn't sure what was right anymore. Slade was gone, buried in a jungle in South America. Sydney was alive. There, just a few feet away, and wonder of wonders, the woman actually wanted him.

She knew about his darkness. About the sins that marked his soul, but she still wanted him.

He would die for her.

So he followed her up the steps to the home that she'd once loved so much, before her family had passed away and left her alone. She opened the door for him. Light spilled out onto the porch.

Onto her.

There would be no going back.

The wooden porch creaked beneath his feet. Her hand was up, reaching for him, and Gunner was pretty sure he'd had this same dream before. Only then, he'd wakened alone, sweating and tangled in his sheets, with her name on his lips.

Make this good for her. Give her pleasure.

Because he only wanted Sydney to know pleasure. She'd known too much pain in her life.

He crossed the threshold with her. Pushed the door shut behind them.

Her breath came a little too fast, and she shifted from her right foot to her left. He'd been in this house before. It carried her sweet scent, light vanilla, and he knew just where her bedroom waited.

Down the hallway, second door on the right.

Could he make it that far?

"Gunner…"

He loved the way she said his name. Breathless. Eager.

Can't make it that far. He'd done well to make it out of the street and into her house.

Gunner pulled Sydney against him, breathed in that vanilla scent and locked his hands around her waist. Those jeans had been driving him crazy. "I—I can't go slow."

"Good."

She surprised him. Always.

Then his mouth was on hers. He thrust his tongue past her lips, and she was the sweetest thing he'd ever tasted.

Before, he'd told himself to stay hands-off, but in Mexico, when she'd walked away and hadn't looked back, he'd realized that she was too important to lose.

Now his hands were most definitely *on* her.

Her breasts were pressed against his chest. Her hips arched against him. He wanted her naked. He wanted to kiss every inch of her.

And he would. The second time.

The first time—the time that *should* have been perfect—need was controlling him. Raw lust.

So he stripped her. He couldn't take his mouth from hers. His hands learned her body and slid over her silken flesh even as he shoved down her jeans.

He heard her kick off the sandals that had made him ache. He would have liked for her to keep them on—*another time*.

Then they were falling together onto her sofa. He was kissing her neck now, inhaling more of that wonderful scent, even as his hands went between her thighs. He meant to pull away her panties, but his fingers were too rough and the silk tore.

Sydney just laughed.

He loved her laugh.

After Peru, it had taken too long for her laugh to come back.

No. He slammed the door on that thought and instead enjoyed the soft heat of her flesh. She was pushing up against him, whispering his name.

His head lifted. He stared at her and told her the simple truth, "You are the most beautiful thing I've ever seen."

Her lips curled in a smile.

Take.

He yanked open his jeans, pushed his body deeper between her thighs. Waited right there at the entrance to her body. This was the moment. No going back. No—

She arched toward him, and he sank inside her.

The pleasure was so incredible that he had to clench his teeth together to hold back a groan. Nothing, *nothing,* had ever felt so good.

Or so right.

He began to thrust. Withdrawing slowly, then plunging back inside her. She was paradise to him, the best dream he'd ever had, and he kissed as much of her body as he could.

Her nipples were tight, pink, and when he licked one, she tensed beneath him.

Gunner felt the pleasure rock through her.

Her legs lifted, locked around his hips. Then she started pushing up with her hips.

He couldn't hold back. His own thrusts became even harder. He caught her hands and laced his fingers with hers.

He stared into her eyes.

Saw her climax. Her green gaze went wide, then wild as the pleasure crested through her.

His release swept him away on a wave so intense that he

shuddered and pushed deeper into her. The release shook his whole body. Seemed to gut him and never end.

I don't want it to end.

He wanted to keep holding her to make the perfect moment last as long as possible.

He kissed her again because he needed to taste her pleasure, to taste all of her.

And he swore that before the night was done, he would.

Chapter Two

The ringing of her phone woke Sydney. Her hand flew out automatically, reaching for her nightstand—for the phone. But instead of scooping up her phone, her fingers collided with warm, strong flesh.

Not a dream.

Her eyes snapped open, and she found herself staring straight into Gunner's dark gaze. There was no sleepiness in that gaze, just a deep hunger.

For her.

Then he reached out and grabbed the ringing phone from her nightstand. Silently, he handed it to her.

"S-Sydney Sloan." Her fingers tightened around the phone. Gunner's tanned fingers were sliding down her arm.

Goose bumps rose on her flesh as she remembered the night before. The things he'd done to her. What she'd done to him.

More, please.

"Sydney?" Logan barked. "Sydney, are you okay?"

She shot up in bed, clutching the sheet to her chest. "I'm fine. Just…sleeping." Gunner didn't stop stroking her. He raised himself, and his lips brushed over her shoulder.

She shivered.

"Look, I know you were due to have a few weeks off, but

we've got a case that we can't refuse. I've got you booked on a jet to Peru at three today."

Peru.

"I'm going to call Gunner and Cale. They'll be meeting up with you there."

I can tell Gunner. He's right here kissing me, lying naked next to me. She cleared her throat. "What's the case?" She hadn't been back to Peru in two years. Not since Slade had died in that jungle, and the place had nearly become her own grave, too.

"An American is being held hostage by a group of rebels."

Hostage rescue. That was what their team did best.

"He needs us," Logan said. "So be on that plane."

"I'll be there," she whispered, and then, because Logan would figure the situation out when he had to make reservations for Gunner—and those flight reservations had Gunner leaving from Baton Rouge, Sydney said, "Now hold on, and I'll get Gunner for you."

Gunner's gaze rose to hers. She knew that her cheeks flushed; she could feel the burn. But this wasn't the time for secrets. They had a case to work. And when a civilian's life was on the line, there wasn't room for embarrassment.

Gunner took the phone from her but didn't look away from her eyes. "Gunner."

There was a beat of silence. Then Sydney rolled away from Gunner and climbed from the bed before she could overhear Logan's response to the discovery that Gunner was so close she could just, ahem, hand him her phone first thing in the morning.

She grabbed for a robe. Her body ached in a way that felt so good, and she hated that their time together was already ending.

No, not ending. They were just beginning. They'd turned a corner last night, and there would be no going back for them.

"I'll be there," she heard Gunner say, and she looked up as he ended the call.

No man should look as sexy as he did. His hair was a little tousled. A line of stubble coated his square jaw, and his eyes blazed as they raked over her.

"We have at least six hours," Gunner told her.

Six hours.

She nodded.

"I want you."

Her fingers clenched around the belt of the robe. "Again?"

"Always."

She dropped the robe and climbed back in bed with him. Six hours.

This was perfect. What she'd hoped for.

And this time, things would end well for her in Peru. She wouldn't lose Gunner. Not the way that she'd lost Slade.

Gunner's lips pressed to hers, and she shoved away the fear that wanted to rise within her.

Peru. The last time she'd been to Peru, her lover had died there.

It won't happen this time. She'd finally gotten her chance with Gunner. It wouldn't slip through her fingers.

LOGAN STARED DOWN at the phone in his hand. Gunner was with Sydney.

He'd seen the sexual awareness between the two of them. Had known that Gunner wanted Sydney, and that the sniper had held back with her. He had clung so tightly to his control and his rule that Sydney was off-limits.

But it looked as if Gunner had broken his rule.

Logan tossed aside the phone and stared at the photographs in front of him. The tip he'd received could be wrong. He shouldn't *want* it to be wrong, but he did.

Because Gunner was his friend. Gunner had been through hell. The man deserved some happiness.

But if the intel was right—and this intel had come right down from Bruce Mercer, the man who'd formed the EOD—then Gunner's life was about to be ripped apart.

"Enjoy her while you can," Logan whispered. Because Gunner would need some good memories to hold tight to in the darkness that was coming.

PERU WAS JUST as hot and beautiful and wild as Sydney remembered. When the plane touched down, and she headed out on the tarmac, the heat was the first thing to hit her.

Cale was inside the airport, waiting for them. Gunner walked right beside Sydney, his hand lightly pressing at the base of her back.

To any onlookers, they probably looked like a vacationing couple.

That was their cover, after all. Lovers. A cover they'd used before.

Only this time, they weren't pretending.

When they entered the airport, Cale approached them with a broad grin. Again, another cover. The reuniting friends. He slapped Gunner on the back and hugged Sydney.

"Ready?" he asked quietly, keeping his smile in place.

She always was.

They went outside together and tossed their bags into the back of Cale's jeep.

Sydney climbed into the front seat next to Cale, while Gunner jumped in the back. In moments, Cale was driving them away from the airport.

"Where's Logan?" Gunner asked, his voice rising over

the growl of the engine. "I thought he was meeting us down here."

"He's doing recon," Cale said, keeping his eyes on the road. Cale was an ex–Army Ranger, one who'd actually been targeted by the EOD for takedown.

He'd been framed for the murders of three EOD agents. He'd proven his innocence and earned his way onto their team.

"Have you seen a picture of the target?" Sydney asked. She was trying hard not to glance back at Gunner, but she was so aware of him. She was hyperaware of every single move that he made.

Had they really spent the night together? She'd wanted him for so long that part of her wondered if it had all just been a wonderful dream.

An erotic dream.

She couldn't help herself—she glanced back at him.

And found Gunner's dark eyes locked on her.

There was such heat in that gaze. She swallowed and forced her eyes away from him as Cale said—

"No, I haven't seen any visuals on him yet. I just know that the order for extraction came down from the top."

She caught the brief grin that flashed over Cale's face.

"Seems Mr. Mercer thinks this rescue is priority, and he wanted *only* the Shadow Agents to take point on this one."

The Shadow Agents. Sure, there were other teams in the EOD, but *their* team had earned the moniker of Shadow Agents because of the way they handled their missions. They went in soundlessly and attacked before their enemies even realized they were there. Then they vanished, disappearing like shadows.

Gunner was especially good at being a shadow. If Gunner didn't want you to know he was there, you wouldn't.

Sydney knew Gunner's grandfather had been the one to

first train him to track and hunt on a reservation. Gunner was the best hunter she'd ever seen, even better than Slade.

Slade's body was in Peru. That knowledge was sitting heavily on her now that she was back in the area.

The EOD had tried to recover his remains again and again, but the rebels they'd fought that day had taken his body away from the scene. Despite the EOD's efforts, they hadn't been able to bring him home.

Slade had a grave, an empty one, one that honored him as the soldier he'd been. But he'd actually never made it back home.

"Logan told me that you and Gunner had been in Peru before," Cale said.

She cleared her throat. "A…few times."

"Logan has set us up in a resort near the beach. You and Gunner are supposed to look like honeymooners."

Because sometimes it wasn't about hiding in a hut or sliding through the jungle. Blending in plain sight could work so much better. The EOD knew this well.

"And I'm your single friend, enjoying some R & R myself." The road was bumpy and the jeep bounced. Once, twice. "Sure is a long way from Texas," he murmured, and she heard the faint drawl in his voice.

Cale's home was in Texas, and the EOD agent he'd replaced—Jasper—was currently living in Texas with Cale's sister.

"When are we looking at extraction?" Gunner asked as he leaned forward. His fingers were on the back of Sydney's seat. It almost felt as if he was playing with her hair. Was he?

"Logan said this was a fast-moving mission. We want the civilian out of there within twenty-four hours."

Sydney nodded. Definitely doable. As soon as Logan returned, she'd start her own reconnaissance work. She could uplink to satellites and get aerial maps of the area to find the best places for them to venture in as they started the rescue operation. As long as she had a good computer and the necessary uplink, she'd be able to access anything that the team needed. Tech had always been her specialty.

Then the jeep turned and headed through the high gates of the resort. Sydney put a smile on her face. She could pretend to be a happy honeymooner. With Gunner at her side, she could do anything.

And she *was* happy, even if painful memories were trying to push their way into her mind. Peru had been a nightmare for her once, but it didn't have to be again.

The valet hurried over to the jeep. Gunner was already out and reaching for Sydney. His hand curled around hers, swallowing her fingers. His hold was strong, possessive. And the kiss that he brushed over her lips—it felt possessive, too.

Just for show…or was that something more?

Cale was laughing and saying something, playing his part. Gunner responded, but Sydney was lost.

She actually wished that this moment could be real. That she was just a happy honeymooner. A woman with Gunner.

But this wasn't her life. She had a mission. A rescue. A civilian who needed her. She'd get the job done.

She'd get her man, too.

Gunner's arm wrapped around Sydney's shoulders. He steered her toward the entrance to the resort. She took a deep breath and slipped into her role.

LOGAN'S BODY WAS pressed tightly to the ground. He kept only his head up as he peered through the binoculars to get a visual on the small camp that sat at the base of the mountain. Not a typical rebel group, from what he'd been able to tell. These guys were armed to the teeth, patrol-

ling constantly, and that one tent to the back...the one that
housed the hostage...

There'd been no movement from that tent for the past
four hours. Logan knew that fact for certain, because he'd
been unmoving in his own position for that time.

He shouldn't have come out alone, he knew that, but before he brought Sydney out there, before Gunner got the
rebels in his sights, Logan just had to be sure of his target.

An armed guard headed toward the tent, lifted the flap,
and went inside. Logan stopped breathing.

Then the guard came out again, leading the hostage. Logan's fingers tightened around the binoculars as he stared
at that prisoner. Long hair and a beard that hadn't been
trimmed in what looked like months. The man was walking with a faint limp.

This wasn't a hostage who had been taken a few days
ago. This was a man who had been held for a very, very
long time.

Logan stared at the man's face.

And knew the mission was going to be personal.

GUNNER TIPPED THE bellman and shut the door. Then he
flipped the lock and turned his attention to Sydney.

She stood in front of a big bed, her blond hair framing
her face. Her eyes were wide and fixed on him, but she
wasn't smiling.

Sydney looked nervous. An unusual situation for her. As
far as he knew, Sydney was never nervous.

He took a step toward her, and she tensed.

What the hell? "Sydney?"

She shook her head. Then she smiled and gave the light
laugh that always made his chest ache. "I swear, I feel like
I'm on a real honeymoon."

If only. He wouldn't say he hadn't thought about what

it would be like to marry her, because he had. Too many times. Even when she'd been planning to marry his brother, he'd thought—

She should be mine.

Then Slade had died, and he'd hated himself for the jealousy he'd felt.

"Are you…are you okay with being back here again?" Sydney asked him quietly.

He strolled toward the window, then looked out over the lush resort. Within the resort's walls, everything was beautiful, perfect. But there were other parts of Peru that were savage. Dangerous. Once you left the city and journeyed into the jungle, civilization truly faded away. "I've been back here a few times since his death."

"You have?" Surprise lifted her words.

He knew she'd stayed away. But he'd had to come back. "I tried to find him." Again and again. "My grandfather would have wanted him brought back." *I wanted him back.* He shrugged, trying to push away the past. "But I couldn't find Slade."

The floor creaked behind him, and then Sydney's soft hands were on his shoulders, curling over him. Her touch was warm, soft, and he remembered all the ways that she had touched him during their night together. The ways he'd touched her.

The ways he would touch her again.

He had Sydney now, and he didn't plan to let her go. Gunner turned toward her. His fingers skimmed over the curve of her cheek. He'd spent the past two years guarding her, determined to protect her from any danger that came their way.

Because Sydney seemed drawn to the danger.

She was the strongest woman he'd ever met, and her brain—hell, the things the lady could do with a computer amazed him. She'd been in the air force, he knew that. A lieutenant colonel. So in addition to her computer skills, there was no plane the woman couldn't fly. She'd flown their team out of more than a few hot spots around the world.

Slade had been a pilot, too. Not in the air force, though. His brother had done a stint in the army, then gotten civilian flying lessons after his tour of duty.

On a charter run to South America, Slade's plane had crashed in the wrong spot at the wrong time.

Against orders, Sydney and Gunner had gone in after him.

But they'd failed to bring him home.

"Gunner?" Her voice was soft.

He'd pulled her out of the jungle in Peru. He'd been so afraid she'd die on him. Her blood had stained his hands. She'd shuddered and jerked, cried out desperately.

For Slade.

But Gunner had been the one there for her. He'd always be there for her.

He offered her a smile, when he wasn't normally the type to smile. He wasn't like Cale or Logan. They could flirt and charm at will. He knew he had a dangerous edge. One that frightened more than it charmed.

But Sydney didn't seem frightened. He shook his head and asked, "Why?"

She blinked; then her blond eyebrows rose in confusion.

"Why me?" he asked her. He should have probably just kept quiet, but, hell, he was no prize. His body was scarred…sliced open, literally. He'd been caught by the enemy more times than he wanted to count. And during one bloody, pain-filled capture, he'd been sure that death would take him.

His captors had tied him up and come at him with a

knife. They'd wanted information. He hadn't given it to them, so they'd sliced him over and over on his stomach, his chest. Cuts meant to break him.

But he'd gotten away.

They'd died.

There was nothing light or easy about him—nothing safe.

So why in the hell did Sydney want to be with him? She could have anyone.

"What do you mean?" Sydney still seemed confused.

She was so beautiful. Fragile, though that delicacy was a deception, he knew.

"Why was it me…and not someone else?" Not that guy in the bar who'd had his hands all over her. Sydney could have taken another lover over the past two years. She hadn't. He knew because he always watched her too closely.

If she had tried to take another lover, what would he have done?

Better not think about it.

With her, his control could be a delicate thing. If she'd actually turned to another, Gunner wasn't sure that his control would have lasted. That *other* guy would have found himself in a battle.

"I'm with you because you remind me that I'm alive." Her smile seemed bittersweet. "When I'm with you, I feel. I want. I need."

He felt too much when he was with her. That was dangerous—for them both.

"I don't like being back here," she told him quietly, "but I'm glad that I'm with you." She rose onto her toes. Her lips brushed over his. "I've wanted to be with you for a long time."

He'd been rough with her before, so hungry and desperate. This time, before the mission started, he was determined to use care with her. She deserved care.

Gunner lifted her up. Held her in his arms and then took her to that big, giant bed. He laid her down, slowly stripped her, kissed every inch of flesh that was revealed to him, and he kept a stranglehold on his control.

This time, he'd show her the way things were supposed to be between them. This time, it would all be for her.

He kissed her breasts, loving the tight peaks of her nipples. Like candy. So good and sweet and perfect for his mouth. Her stomach dipped down, and he explored all of her, sliding his fingers gently over her skin, over her sensitive core.

She arched against him, whispering his name.

He kept touching her, kissing and enjoying the silken feel of her skin.

"Gunner, *I want you.*"

Those were the words he needed. He'd never be a stand-in for a ghost, but Sydney wasn't asking for a stand-in. She wanted him.

He pulled away from her just long enough to push down his jeans. Then he positioned his body between her thighs. One strong thrust—*yes*—and he drove into her, pleasure pulsing along his aroused length.

Her legs wrapped around him. She urged him to thrust deeper, harder, and he gave in to her. Moving quickly, wanting to give her as much pleasure as she could stand, wanting to give her everything.

When her body tensed beneath his, he knew her release was close. His spine tingled, his body tightened, but he forced himself to hold back.

He needed to feel her pleasure first.

Then she was gasping, calling his name, and her nails were scoring his shoulders. The pleasure washed across her face, brightening her eyes and flushing her cheeks.

Only then did he give in to his own need. He drove into her and let go.

The climax ripped through him, just as strong as the pleasure he'd gotten the night before.

He'd always known that Sydney was a dangerous woman, but he hadn't realized that once he'd had a taste of the paradise she offered, there would be no turning back.

THE RAP SOUNDED on their door an hour later. Gunner glanced up to see Sydney coming out of the shower. Her hair was still wet, and her clothes clung tightly to her body.

"Must be Cale...or Logan," she said, glancing toward the door.

Logan would know what they'd been up to. Even though they'd tried to fix the wrecked bed, Gunner knew that the minute Logan looked into his eyes, he would know.

Logan was his friend, and the man could read him too well.

Logan also knew well enough not to say a damn word that would make Sydney feel uncomfortable.

Gunner rose and headed for the door. He checked through the peephole and saw Logan staring straight ahead. After opening the door, Gunner stepped back so that Logan could enter.

Their team leader stalked inside, his body tight with tension.

Frowning, Gunner locked the door behind him.

"Did you get a visual?" Sydney asked as she approached him.

Logan gave a grim nod.

Then Gunner saw Logan's gaze sweep from Sydney, to the bed, to Gunner.

Logan's stare was…guarded. No emotion.

Gunner's gut clenched.

"Is Cale coming in for the update?" Sydney glanced toward the door. "I'm sure he needs to hear—"

"I need to talk to the two of you first." Logan's words were emotionless. Just like his eyes.

Gunner didn't like where this scene was going.

"Mercer…Mercer is the one who handed down this job. He asked *specifically* for our team to handle the mission."

"We are the best," Sydney said, grinning a bit.

Logan didn't smile. "He had a tip about the hostage, and he wanted us to follow up. *I* wanted to get a visual before I passed on the suspicions to the team."

"Just what kind of suspicions are we talking about?" Gunner crossed his hands over his chest and waited.

Sydney came to his side. Her grin was gone. Her shoulders brushed against his.

Logan's watchful gaze noted that light touch. His eyes narrowed, and he blew out a hard breath. "Mercer had intel that an American pilot was being held. A man with strong ties that could potentially be…manipulated by the group holding him."

"What kind of ties?" Sydney asked.

"Military ties to a covert team." Logan's shoulders straightened. "To *our* team."

Gunner's heartbeat kicked up.

"I saw the hostage earlier." Logan's hands were clenched. That wasn't a good sign. Not good at all. His gaze came back to Gunner. "I got the visual confirmation that we needed."

Why wasn't he just coming out and *saying*—

"The hostage...it's Slade."

Sydney's body swayed next to him, and Gunner automatically reached out, wrapping his hands around her shoulders.

Then he froze.

Slade?

"He's thinner. His hair's longer. He's got a beard and a limp but...*it's him.*"

"Slade is dead." Sydney's voice was hushed.

Logan's gaze drifted to her. "No, he's not."

"We *buried* him."

Gunner felt like ice was wrapping around him. "We put a tombstone over an empty grave." He stepped toward Logan. "I saw him die. I was there." This couldn't be happening. "There was no pulse," he growled out the words. "I checked. There was no surviving the hits that Slade had taken. With that much blood loss..."

He'd been dead.

Because Gunner never would have left him if he thought his brother had still been alive.

"I saw him, Gunner. I. Saw. Him." Now Logan raked a hand through his hair, and Gunner realized just how agitated the team leader was. "The features are the same. Hell, I'm not one hundred percent on this...we'd need DNA for that...but the intel Mercer has...what I just saw...it *looks* like him."

"G-Gunner?" Sydney sounded shocked. Lost.

He couldn't look at her right then. Because he was afraid of what he might see in her eyes.

He'd had her beneath him on that bed, been inside her...

While his brother had been held captive in a camp.

Slade's fiancée.

"We're going to do more recon tonight. We don't have

time to waste. We need to use the darkness while we can," Logan said. His voice was stiff. "Syd, I'll need you to get working on the satellite imagery. We'll all go in to sweep the area. Then we'll plan for extraction at 0600."

Extraction.

His brother's extraction.

The silence in the room was too heavy.

"Gunner, I want to talk to you alone." Logan's words held the snap of command.

And Gunner realized he was staring at Logan, but seeing nothing.

But he gave a rough nod and turned toward the room's door. He brushed by Sydney—*can't look at her yet, can't*—because he didn't want to see the regret in her eyes.

She loved Slade, not him, and to find out that he might still be alive, after everything, had to be tearing her apart.

Logan shut the door after them. They were in the hallway. Alone. There was no sound from the room behind him.

Nothing at all.

"You gonna be able to handle this?" Logan whispered.

This? Finding my brother? Losing Sydney? Gunner nodded. "I'll get the mission done."

Logan grabbed his arm. "I saw the way you looked at her. I know you were *with* her in Baton Rouge." His voice was a bare whisper of sound. "Man, I'm so damn sorry."

Sorry that Slade was alive? They should be celebrating that miracle. Sydney would be celebrating.

And Gunner *was* glad. His brother's death had weighed on him for two years. They'd fought just before Slade's plane went down. Fought because…Slade knew how Gunner felt for Sydney.

Gunner had known that Slade didn't deserve her. He'd caught his brother cheating on Sydney, twice. He'd threatened to tell her the truth.

"You don't deserve her." That had been his snarl to Slade. But the truth was...

Neither of us deserved her.

But it looked as if one of them would still get her.

"Mercer wanted you on this mission because Slade's your blood, but the boss didn't know about you and Sydney—"

"There is no me and Sydney." He forced himself to say the words. There couldn't be a he and Sydney. Not now. Maybe after the mission, maybe after—

Stop lying to yourself.

His dream had ended, just as he'd known it would. But he'd just wanted more time with her.

More.

"Gunner..."

He shrugged away from Logan's hold. "We'll do the mission. We'll get him out—if he's Slade, if he's someone else...we'll get him out, either way." Because that was what they did.

The mission.

Always.

He hated the pity in Logan's eyes. He'd rather have seen the guarded mask come back.

"She wants you," Logan said.

Gunner stiffened. "She wanted to marry him."

Maybe it's not him. But Logan wouldn't have said that he thought it was, not unless the evidence he had was compelling.

Logan exhaled on a rough sigh. "We go out in an hour."

Gunner's head jerked in a nod.

"Gunner—"

He held up his hand. "Let's just get him free." That was all he could think right now. Do the mission. Save the hostage.

Let everything else go to hell.

"Okay." Logan's sigh was rough. "But you're to stand back on the actual extraction, got it? You'll provide the cover for the team."

The way he always did. Shooting, killing, from a distance.

"I'll need you and Syd to survey the area more. When I left, it looked like they were bringing in more men." He paused. "Are you going to stay in control?"

Sydney was the only one who could make him lose control. Sydney...who wasn't his.

"Yes." He didn't want the word to be a lie.

And maybe it wouldn't be.

He didn't walk back into the room with Sydney then. He walked down the hallway, went outside.

I shouldn't have touched her. I should have stayed away.

Because now—now he knew what he'd be losing.

What he'd lose, even as he found his brother again.

I'm sorry, Slade. Because he'd just taken the one thing that his brother loved most.

HER EAR WAS pressed to the door. The resort might be fancy, but the room doors were thin, and Sydney could hear every word that Gunner and Logan said.

There is no me and Sydney.

The words hurt her, pounding through the numbness that had surrounded her ever since Logan had said that Slade might be alive.

Alive? How was that even possible? Gunner had been so sure that he was dead, and she'd seen Slade's injuries. Too many injuries. Too much blood.

Slade had been dead. She'd been sure of it. If he hadn't been...

We left him alone? For two years?

A tear trekked down her cheek, and once more, she heard Gunner's gruff words echo through her mind.

There is no me and Sydney.

Chapter Three

Gunner wouldn't look at her. Sydney crept quietly through the jungle, stepping so that she wouldn't so much as snap a twig, and she was too aware of the silence that came from the man behind her.

Cale and Logan were scouting on the west side of the area. She and Gunner were alone on the east side. The chirps and calls from the insects and creatures in the dark jungle drifted in the air.

And no sound came from Gunner.

She stopped. Took a deep breath, and turned to face him. "Say *something*."

The moon shone down on him, but she couldn't read his expression. Like Logan, Gunner was too skilled at hiding what he felt.

"Are you happy? Stunned? Talk to me!" Didn't he realize that he was her best friend? When she had a secret to share with someone, she always went to him.

He was her rock.

Her…lover.

Slade's alive.

"It was a mistake," Gunner told her.

Her heart slammed into her chest. "You don't think it's Slade?" Her voice was quiet, so she stepped closer to him.

So close that she could feel the seductive warmth of his body. "Logan's wrong and—"

"We were a mistake."

Her body trembled, but she kept her chin up. She kept her eyes on him only because she *wouldn't* break there, not in the jungle. Not in front of him. "Is that really how you feel?"

She didn't feel that way. Being with him had been the only thing that seemed right in her world.

Something that felt so amazing, no, it couldn't be a mistake.

"It won't happen again. We won't be together again."

A bullet wound would probably hurt less. Actually, she knew from personal experience that it would. "It might not even be him." Her hoarse voice. But it was true. She'd given up on Slade, put him to rest and moved on.

"And if it is?" Now Gunner was the one to take a step toward her. "I *left* him. I thought he was dead. If he was alive, for all this time, do you know the hell he would have been put through by his captors?"

She didn't want to think too much about that. She *couldn't* think about it now.

"I'm his older brother. I was supposed to keep him safe." Disgust tightened his mouth. "Not screw his fiancée."

Pinpricks of heat shot across her cheeks. "Is that what you did? Because I thought we'd been making love."

Her mistake.

"We need to finish scouting so we can secure the area. "Now isn't the time to talk about this."

Right. Of course. But would there ever be a time when he wanted to talk? "It was more to me," she said, and turned away.

That was when she realized…all of the chirps and calls had stopped. The jungle was eerily silent around them, and clouds were starting to drift across the surface of the moon, making the shadows even darker.

Sydney brought up her weapon, and she knew Gunner was doing the same. She stepped forward, her body tensing now. Something had changed in the jungle. Shifted.

She and Gunner had been hunting before, but now she had the feeling that they were the prey.

The rebel camp should have been about a mile away. No one should be in their immediate area.

But the brush was so thick and heavy.

Sweat coated Sydney's back and slicked her fingers as she held her weapon.

Then she heard it. The snap of a twig. Twenty feet to the left. She swung around with her gun.

Another twig snapped.

That snapping came from thirty feet to the right.

Trouble.

She felt, rather than saw, Gunner's movements as he swung to the right. One word whispered through her mind: *surrounded.*

Her breath barely left her lungs. She reached up with her left hand and tapped the communicator near her ear. "Alpha One…" Her words were a whisper as she signaled Logan. "We've got movement in our perimeter. There's—"

Footsteps thundered toward them, coming fast and hard. She took aim, ready to shoot, but then she saw the hostage. A man who was being pushed through the jungle, with some kind of brown sack over his head. His hands were bound in front of him, and a gun was pressed to the top right side of that sack, just where his temple would be. A flashlight was held on the man, the better for them to see just what trump card the captors held.

"Deje caer sus armas!" The shout came from the man who held the gun. *Drop your weapons.*

Sydney took aim at him. *"Deje caer sus armas!"* She snarled right back at him.

He wasn't alone. There was another armed man who'd come out from the right side. Sydney had heard his rushing footsteps. Gunner hadn't fired on him, because, like her, he had to be worried about the hostage.

An innocent getting injured in a firefight wasn't on the agenda.

But neither was getting captured.

A radio crackled behind her. The other man was calling for backup. If they didn't do something, soon, this mission was about to go bad.

I shouldn't have gotten distracted. This is my fault. I should have kept walking, kept searching the area. But I was too caught up in Gunner.

Now they were both in trouble.

The man near the hostage laughed and shook his head. *"Voy a disparar contra él."*

I will shoot him. Yes, she'd just bet that he'd shot plenty of men in his time.

"Please!" The broken cry came from the hostage. "Help me!"

"We will," Sydney promised him, but she wasn't dropping her gun yet.

Only...a weapon *did* hit the ground. She turned at the thud. Gunner had tossed away his gun. His hands were up. What was he doing? Surrender wasn't the way the team operated.

"Sydney?" It was Cale's voice in her ear. If she could hear him, Gunner could, too. They were all on the same comm link. "We're coming for you."

But would he come soon enough?

Gunner walked forward, putting his body before her.

Sydney didn't know if he was protecting her or blocking her shot, but either way, the result was the same.

"No dispare," Gunner said, voice loud and carrying easily. With the transmitter so close to his mouth, Cale would hear every word and understand exactly what was happening to them. *"Puede tener tres rehenes en lugar de dos."*

Don't shoot. You can have three hostages instead of two.

That was a terrible plan.

But then she felt the cold metal of a gun being shoved against the base of her neck.

It looked as though it was their only plan, for the moment.

Sydney let her weapon drop, and she lifted her hands in surrender.

Cale, hurry up, she thought.

Because she wasn't sure how much time they had.

HE'D MADE A deadly mistake.

Gunner sat in the old chair, his hands tied behind him, his ankles lashed to the wooden chair legs. A heavy black sack covered his head. When he strained his eyes, he could just make out a form across from him. The shadowy outline of— "Sydney?" he rasped.

"Yes."

He'd been distracted by her in the jungle. Too aware of her every move. He should have been on the lookout for the enemy, but they'd gotten the drop on him.

On Sydney. As if they were both rookies.

Now the hostage was gone, taken to another tent, and he and Sydney were about to be interrogated.

The last time he'd been interrogated in a South American jungle, he'd had to spend six hours getting enough stitches to close all of the wounds in his body.

Those stitches had been given to him by a relief worker

on the edge of a river. There'd been no anesthesia. He'd roared at the pain.

And called Sydney's name.

Something he'd never told her. What would have been the point?

"It was his voice," Gunner growled as he yanked against his bonds. "You know it was him." There were guards right outside their tent. Guards who'd foolishly thought that they'd taken all of his weapons.

Not that Gunner needed a weapon to kill. He was very good with his hands.

As his last interrogators had discovered.

"I—I can't remember his voice." Her words were soft. Sad. "It's been too long for me, Gunner."

He stilled. That *had* been his brother's voice, hadn't it? Because if it hadn't, then he'd dropped his gun for no damn reason.

I could have taken them out. But he wouldn't have been able to do it without hurting the hostage. If that had been his brother, then Slade had already been hurt enough. Gunner wasn't going to add to the man's pain.

Gunner cleared his throat. "Are you bound?"

"Tied like a pig, with a sack over my head."

He'd thought so, but they'd been separated on the way to the camp. Then he hadn't heard her voice for a while, and he'd...worried. "We're gonna get out of here." His comm transmitter was gone. Taken and smashed in the jungle, just as hers had been.

But this camp wasn't in the location that they'd been told of. Either Logan had been given bad intel or the group had a second and, from the sound of things, much larger base. Because they'd walked east. Been dumped into the back of a vehicle, and they'd zigged and zagged through the jungle before they'd stopped.

Good thing he and Sydney were both equipped with a special GPS locator, courtesy of Uncle Sam. They both had trackers inserted just beneath their skin. Cale and Logan would be able to find them; it was just a matter of time.

"We'll get out of here," Gunner told her as he twisted his wrists. The ropes were rough, and he could feel them tearing into his skin. So what if he got cut? The blood would just make it easier for him to break loose.

Then he heard voices outside. The group leader's voice—that would be the one who'd come for them in the jungle. The one who'd held the hostage and laughed as he stared into Gunner's eyes.

"Sounds like the fun is about to start," Sydney said. There was no fear in her voice. She could have been terrified, and he wouldn't have known. She was in her mission mode now.

"We'll get out of here." He needed her to understand that.

He heard the rustle of the tent's opening. Footsteps came closer. He listened carefully and counted the tread of those footsteps…two men.

One man went to stand behind him.

The other— "You shouldn't have come into my jungle." Heavily accented English, and Gunner knew it was the leader. The guy was standing right in front of him. He could make out the outline of the man's body through the fabric of the sack that covered him.

He could see the guy's body and see the weapon that the man lifted and pointed toward Sydney. "Coming here was a terrible mistake for you both."

"Stop!" Gunner barked, heart racing.

Laughter. Low. Sinister. From the man with the gun. The rebel behind Gunner didn't make a sound.

Rebels…what cause were they fighting for? As far as he

could tell, Logan thought this group was little more than drug runners. Weapons dealers.

"I am not going to shoot the señorita yet. Not just yet." But he still had the weapon near her head. "First, you talk, *sí?* You tell me all about your team. About the men who think they can come into my jungle and take what is mine."

The rope cut deeper into Gunner's wrists. "There is no team. Just us."

Silence. Then, "I can start by shooting her in the knee, if you want."

"There is no team!" Sydney snapped at him.

But Gunner didn't speak. The man's words were replaying in his head. *I can start by shooting her in the knee.*

"You both wore…what are they? Ah…transmitters of some sort. That means you were talking to someone else."

"There is no team," Gunner said woodenly, because that was the response he had to give. When the enemy caught you, you didn't turn. You didn't reveal your intel, and you didn't jeopardize the others still out in the field.

"So sad." Now the man's voice had deepened. Behind him, Gunner heard the other rebel shifting from foot to foot. "He must not care for you at all, señorita."

Gunner yanked on the ropes. They weren't giving. Not yet.

"I don't like hurting women. It's not in my nature, but…" A regretful sigh drifted in the air. "If I do not learn what I must know, there will be no choice for me."

"Let her go!" Gunner demanded as fury swirled inside him. "That's the only choice you need to make."

"No, I need to know about your team. About your… EOD."

Gunner's mind whirled. The rebel—no way should he have known about the Elite Ops Division. They were off the books for a reason.

Classified cases. Classified kills.

"How many EOD agents are in Peru?"

"I don't know what the EOD is," Gunner told him.

A growl broke from the man behind him, and Gunner felt the blade of a knife slice through the sack and press right against his throat.

"Ah…I'm afraid my companion is more impatient than I am."

The companion…he'd moved quickly but wasn't getting a reprimand of any sort by the guy Gunner had pegged as the leader. Unusual. Very unusual. Leaders didn't usually like it when someone jumped the gun.

Maybe he isn't the leader.

Maybe the real leader was the man getting ready to slice open his throat.

The man with the knife hadn't said a word, but the other guy kept talking, throwing out, "Her life doesn't matter to you, but what about your own? Care to tell us about the EOD…now?"

"We don't know what you're talking about!" The angry words came from Sydney. "We can't tell you when we don't know!"

Sydney had been trained not to break, too. They'd both learned how to hold out against torture.

But would he really be able to sit there, while Syndey was hurting? If he heard Sydney in pain, Gunner was afraid that his control would shatter.

The ropes began to give way even as the knife blade pressed deeper into his skin.

"We have intel…that is what you call it, *si?* We have intel of our own, and we know who you both are. We lured you to us because we have…interests…who are after the EOD."

Interests? Would that be the same interested party who had sent out hits on the EOD agents in the U.S. a while back?

"You cannot tell, señorita, but your friend's throat is bleeding. There's a knife against his jugular, and if I don't learn what I must know, then I will tell my associate to kill him."

Gunner heard the sound of Sydney's sharply indrawn breath. Then... "Gunner?"

"It's a scratch," he told her, keeping his voice flat. "I do worse than this when I shave in the morning."

The knife pressed harder.

Gunner laughed. "You think this is torture? You boys need to up your game."

"Perhaps we will," the man said, voice snarling. "But I do not think that we need to keep both of you. We already have one hostage, why keep two more?"

Hell. He'd been afraid of this.

Logan and Cale need to hurry the hell up.

"So, which will we eliminate? The lovely lady or the man who thinks he can laugh at death?"

Gunner knew exactly what choice they needed to make. So he laughed again, mocking them, wanting to draw their attention and do anything necessary to ensure Sydney's survival. "You aren't killing us. You're all talk and—"

Blood slid down his neck.

"—and when I get out of here," Gunner continued, voice roughening, "you'll be the ones to die." The words were a promise. "So, what you need to be doing is running, while you still can."

Was the gun still pressed to Sydney's head? He hoped not. He wanted that gun—and the attention of the two men—focused just on him.

He'd buy Sydney as much survival time as he could. Cale and Logan would come, sooner or later. She just had to live until then.

*My fault. I dropped my guard in the jungle. I got dis-
tracted by her. She won't be dying for my mistake.*

"Who is your hostage?" Sydney's voice came, louder and
sharper than he'd expected. She should have stayed quiet.
Didn't she realize what he was trying to do?

"You come into my jungle," their captor said, "trying to
rescue a man you don't even know?"

"It's my job," Sydney snapped.

"You shouldn't have done this job. You should have just
left him to die." There was the rustle of clothing, and Gunner saw the shadow of their captor's body shift. He thought
the man was coming toward him, but—*no*. He heard the
man step closer to Sydney.

And the knife was suddenly gone from Gunner's throat.
The guard's footsteps shuffled behind Gunner as the man
moved back.

They were told, "It's time to lose a hostage. Do you want
a moment to say your goodbyes?"

Both men were near Sydney now. He could see the dark
outlines of their bodies through his mask. "Don't you even
think of killing her!"

"As if you could stop us…"

"It's all right, Gunner," Sydney said at the same time.
"It's all right."

No, it wasn't. They should be turning their attention on
him. Not her. "What kind of coward holds a woman prisoner like this?"

The men didn't speak.

Sydney did. "Gunner, can you close your eyes?"

Because she must have on a covering just like his. She'd
be able to see a little bit, just as he could. And Sydney didn't
want him seeing her die.

"Yes," he said, even as he kept his eyes wide open. This
wasn't happening. He wouldn't let it happen. Not to her.

He yanked on the rope that bound his wrists. Felt it give way. Just. In. Time.

"Thank you," Sydney said softly. "And, Gunner, I—"

An explosion rocked the tent, and Gunner's chair fell to the side. He yanked out with his hands, shattering the chair legs and pulling free from the ropes that bound his legs.

Voices were crying out. Yelling. And more explosions—they sounded like thunder, but he could feel the heat from the blasts—blasted through the camp. Footsteps pounded out of the room. More shouts.

More fire. He could smell the acrid scent.

"Sydney!"

He yanked the sack off his head and rushed to her. She'd fallen back, too, and, at first, he didn't think she was moving at all. Had they killed her before the explosion? Had that sick jerk with the knife hurt her?

But then she groaned, and he saw her hands come up. She'd worked her wrists free, too. Of course she had. That was his Sydney.

He clawed away the ropes that bound her feet and jerked that sack from over her eyes. With his breath heaving, he stared down at her, desperately looking for blood.

Her eyes were wide and bright. As always, she was the most beautiful thing he'd ever seen. He wanted to kiss her so badly that he ached.

Slade's alive.

He swallowed and pulled Sydney to her feet. "What the hell were you doing?" Gunner demanded. "I wanted their attention on me."

She blinked, and some of the brightness seemed to leave her gaze. "Sorry, I was just doing my part to keep you breathing." She bent down and picked up a sharp chunk of wood, one of the remnants from her chair's legs. "You're welcome."

His hold on her left wrist tightened. "Next time, try to keep yourself alive instead." Because to him, she was the priority.

Gunfire burst out into the night then, firing with a *rat-a-tat* that was too familiar to him. "Our backup is here." Just in time. He'd have to thank Cale and Logan with a round of beer later.

After they all got out of that jungle.

First order of business…get better weapons. That wood of Sydney's wouldn't last long. They'd get weapons, then hurry out there to provide support to the other EOD agents.

Moving like shadows, he and Sydney slid to the front of their tent. Their guards were gone. From what Gunner could see, chaos had taken over the camp. Men were running everywhere, shooting wildly.

Cale wouldn't be positioned close, and those shots being fired so wildly from the rebels *wouldn't* hit him. The guy was a sniper, too. Not ex-SEAL like Gunner, but a Ranger sniper who'd survived some of the deadliest places on earth.

Cale's shots were deliberate, timed perfectly. Gunner realized that the explosions had been his handiwork, too. Cale knew far too much about demolitions.

Gunner scanned the area and found his target. Fifteen feet away. The man who was holding up his gun and staring into the jungle, not even glancing around to cover his back.

"I've got you," Sydney said. "Go ahead."

She'd be covering Gunner's back. He knew he could count on her.

He might be a sniper, but he could still handle up close combat just fine. He'd learned those fighting techniques long before he'd let Uncle Sam talk him into being all he could be.

Gunner rushed silently forward. His target never had a chance to fight him, much less to fire his weapon. Gunner swiped out with his hands, an attack designed to take out his opponent, and before the man's body fell, Gunner had the fellow's gun in his hand.

One weapon down.

He looked up, saw that Sydney was close. She gave him a grim nod.

Just then one of the guards ran out of another tent, screaming and aiming his gun at her head.

No. Gunner lifted his gun instantly. Sydney must have read the danger in his eyes because she dropped to the ground, giving him the perfect shot.

But as he fired, another blast thundered.

Two bullets hit the guard, stopping his attack.

Cale? Probably. The other sniper was doing his job and making sure they got out of there alive.

Sydney didn't stand. Instead, she crawled quickly toward the downed man and took his weapon.

Now that they were both better armed, it was time to search. Because they weren't running out of that camp, weren't fleeing. They'd come there for a reason.

Find the hostage. They'd complete their mission.

We're coming, Slade.

Most of the rebels were fleeing. Some jumped into old trucks; others just ran into the jungle. The explosions had scared them. It looked as though they weren't quite up for trading their lives for their cause.

The more of them that left, well, the easier the EOD's mission became. He and Sydney searched the tents, one after the other. Deserted. Burning. No sign of Slade.

But he *had* to be there.

Or…maybe he was close by. Just through the patch of jungle on the right, Gunner could see the outline of old stones. Big, sprawling, the structure looked like some kind of deserted temple.

Sydney was already nodding, because she'd spotted the structure, too. Gunfire erupted behind Gunner, and he turned, firing back. "Go!" he ordered Sydney. If Slade was out there, they had to get to him. He could be hurt, dying…

Gunner saw Logan appear, and the team leader joined the firefight. Sydney rushed toward the temple.

The bullets kept coming. A lucky shot grazed Gunner's left arm, and he clenched his teeth at the flash of pain.

Then he took aim at the men coming for him.

Chapter Four

Sydney's heartbeat echoed in her ears as she ran toward the narrow entrance to what she could only guess was some kind of crumbling temple. Giant slabs of white rock were turned, forming the sloping entrance. But…there was light coming from inside that temple. And where there was light…

Sydney lifted her gun and went in low. She didn't know what kind of angry reception she'd find waiting for her, but she had to do this search and get back to help Gunner. She had to—

A man was tied to a chair, bound, the way she'd been moments before. He looked like the same man she'd seen in the jungle, because he was wearing that same brown sack over his head. A lantern sat near his feet, revealing his old, ragged pants.

She approached him cautiously. No one else appeared to be in the area, but she didn't want to take any chances. She checked every shadowed space, then eased closer to the bound man.

He stiffened as she drew nearer. His sagging head snapped up. "Who's there?" he demanded.

She wanted to say the voice was familiar to her. Gunner had been so sure it was Slade's voice that they'd heard in the jungle. But Sydney just didn't know. The only voice she knew by heart?

Gunner's rough, rumbling drawl.

"I'm here to help you," she whispered to him. She'd shoved that sharp chunk of wood in her belt, and now she pulled it out and began to saw against his binds with it. "Don't move."

But a shudder ran the length of the man's body. "Talk to me again. I know…"

She frowned at him. She should just take off the sack, find out for certain who this man was. But she was afraid.

And she wasn't usually afraid.

"What do you know?" Sydney asked him.

"I know…" A heaving breath. *"You."*

Her makeshift weapon cut through the binds on his wrists. There was no rope on his ankles, and he surged to his feet. As he turned toward her, he yanked off the sack that covered his head. In that dim lantern light, Sydney got her first look at the hostage's face.

The world seemed to slow its spinning.

His hair was longer, his beard heavy, but…those cheekbones. That hawkish nose.

"Sydney…"

He yanked her into his arms. His mouth pressed to hers, and she was so stunned that she couldn't respond, couldn't move at all.

Slade?

He'd been alive. They'd left him, and he'd been…alive. His mouth was hard on hers. So hard.

She pulled back, staring up at him in shock. "Slade?"

She realized the gunfire had stopped. *A good sign…or a very bad one.* Sydney pushed away from Slade and glanced toward that sloping entrance.

A man stood there. Tall, with wide shoulders, armed. A man who'd been watching them.

He stepped forward, and the lantern light spilled onto Gunner. It was too dark for her to see the expression in his eyes, but his body looked tense.

"Slade?" Gunner's voice was hoarse as he lowered his weapon.

Slowly, Slade turned to face his brother. Slade was thinner—*much thinner*—than he'd been before.

Two years.

Gunner began to walk toward Slade with slow, hesitant steps. "I—I thought you were dead."

Slade shuffled toward him, limping slightly.

Gunner lifted his arms to embrace his brother.

Slade drove his fist into Gunner's jaw.

"Slade!" Sydney shouted.

But Slade wasn't stopping. He attacked Gunner, pummeling him with his fists, kicking him with his legs. Again and again.

Gunner didn't fight back. Didn't try to land a blow, didn't try to block any of the attacks. Gunner fell, and Slade kicked his ribs. Driving in hard with his boot-covered feet.

"Stop!" Sydney grabbed Slade's arm. But he swung around and shoved her back, so hard that she slammed into the rough wall behind her.

"Sydney?" Gunner's growl. And he was rising then.

Even as Slade stood over *her* now, with his fist drawn back as if he'd strike her.

He's been through hell. He doesn't realize what he's doing. Sydney cleared her throat. "You have to calm down, Slade."

Gunfire burst again, sounding as if the blasts came from just yards away.

Sydney shook her head and rose fully to her feet. She

kept her gun in her hand. She'd do whatever was necessary to stop the men from tearing each other apart. "We have to get out of here. Do you understand?"

Slade's breaths sawed in and out of his lungs.

"Slade, do you understand?" There wasn't time to waste. The rebels who'd fled before…what if they'd gone out to get reinforcements? Their EOD team was good, but it was just the four of them against a small army.

Slade nodded. "I…understand."

Gunner was on his feet. Blood dripped from his busted lip.

"Then you stay between me and Gunner when we go out of here. You do exactly what we say."

Slade glanced at Gunner. Even in the dark, she could feel Slade's rage.

Rage? At the brother he'd loved so much?

More gunfire. Then…silence.

"Let's go," Sydney whispered. She had to focus on just getting Slade out of there. They'd deal with everything else once they were in a secure location. The temple looked as if it would fall on them all any second. Not secure at all.

She led the men out, and Gunner closed in behind Slade. She searched first, making sure it was clear to run, and then they were moving, rushing forward and staying within the cover of trees as much as possible.

And she saw Logan firing at a man who'd rushed up toward him. The man fell, and Logan kept running, motioning for Sydney and her group to join him.

She was more than happy to follow him out of that place.

They went to the left, to the right, following a trail that only existed in Logan's mind. Then, beneath the hanging vines of a twisted tree, she saw a jeep, half-hidden by the foliage. Logan jumped in the front of the vehicle.

"Get in!" Logan yelled.

She grabbed Slade's arm and helped hoist him inside and as soon as his feet touched down—

Gunner knocked Sydney to the ground. Two *cracks* of gunfire sounded, and a bullet slammed into the jeep, exactly where she had been about two seconds ago.

His gaze bored into hers. The sun was just starting to rise, still not giving her enough light to gauge the expression in his eyes, and she wished that she could see so much more.

Logan returned fire on the enemy.

Gunner hauled her up, shielded her with his body, and all but tossed her into the jeep.

Then Logan was taking off and rushing away from the battle. Yanking on the wheel, finding a road—well, not a road so much, just a space between trees that most would never have known existed.

The jeep slowed for an instant, and Cale jumped from the shadows and slid into the back.

Then they kept going.

Faster, faster.

Until the gunfire sounded like fireworks in the distance. Until Sydney could breathe without tasting smoke.

She looked around her slowly. Gunner was pressed tightly to her side, and he had a hard grip on her wrist, as if he were afraid that she was going to try to get away from him.

Slade was on his other side. Not speaking. Barely seeming to move at all.

She stared down at Gunner's hand. Very slowly, his hold eased.

Then he wasn't holding her at all.

"Slade Ortez?" Logan said as he gripped the steering wheel.

"Yes." A word that barely rose above the roar of the motor.

"You're going to be safe now," Logan told him. "We're going to get you home."

Gunner wasn't touching her now, wasn't looking at anyone.

She frowned at him, and realized that she could smell blood.

Sydney's hands flew over Gunner.

"Stop!" he told her.

She wasn't going to stop touching him because, right there, high on his left shoulder, she'd just felt something wet and sticky. Blood. "You were shot."

His fingers curled around hers. Pushed her hand away. "It's nothing."

Yes, it was a *bullet wound.* Not some nick. "Is the bullet still in you?"

He didn't answer, and that silence *was* an answer for her.

"You deserve more than that!" came Slade's snarling voice. *"Brother."* The word sounded like a curse. "You deserve to die."

Sydney gasped at the words. "Slade, you don't even know what you're saying!" She remembered Gunner shoving her to the ground. The bullet that had hit the side of the jeep. Only…hadn't she heard two shots then? Two shots, but only one bullet had gone into the jeep.

The other bullet had been meant to go in her.

Gunner took a bullet for me.

"I know…exactly…what I'm saying," Slade growled.

No, he didn't. He'd been in captivity. Been hurt, tortured, but the man talking, that *wasn't* the man she knew. "Gunner just risked his life for you."

They all had.

"The bullet has to come out," she whispered to Gunner. She tried to inspect the wound again.

He gave a grim nod. But…he pushed her hand away once more.

The move just hurt.

"When we're secure," Gunner said, no emotion slipping into his voice. "I can handle it 'til then."

Of course he could. Gunner could handle anything. Handle it, and keep on going. Never showing emotion.

While emotions were about to rip her apart.

They didn't immediately head for civilization. If they were being tailed, they didn't want anyone following them.

They changed vehicles. Once. Twice. Logan picked up the emergency cash that had been sent ahead for the mission, and only *then* did they head back for the coast. The sun was rising in the sky, and Sydney glanced over to see the haggard lines on Slade's face.

He'd aged ten years in two.

The laughing man she'd known was gone. He'd never be coming back.

And as for Gunner…

His eyes weren't meeting hers. He talked only when he had to do so, and the scent of his blood was still heavy in the air.

She pulled her gaze from his. The jungle was behind them, the gunfire just a memory. They'd all changed clothes at their last stop. Gunner had shoved a makeshift bandage over his wound, to stop the blood from leaking through to his clothes.

They didn't look as if they'd just spent the night in the jungle. More as if they'd just been partying too much.

Except for Slade. New clothes hadn't been able to change his appearance that much. Gaunt, grizzled. He would need more care than a five-minute pit stop could give him.

They weren't headed back to their original resort. No, she'd made different arrangements for their accommodations postrescue. It was always important to switch bases—the better to throw off the enemy—and she'd planned for the switch.

They were headed to villas now, private villas on the beach. High-end, far away from anything but luxury. Not a place the rebel group should think to look for government agents. And that was why it would be such a perfect hiding spot.

Not that they'd be hiding for long. Soon enough, they'd all be heading back for the U.S.

Logan and Cale took care of getting the keys to the villas. Three of them, all far away from the rest, nestled on a secluded strip of beach.

Slade climbed from the vehicle, and, for a moment, he just stared at that long, stretching coast.

Gunner followed him out, and Sydney caught the faint tremble of his body. *Get the bullet out.* Her gaze met Cale's, and the ex-Ranger gave a quick nod.

They forced Gunner into the first villa. Literally had to drag the guy in.

But they got him in.

"I can handle this!" Gunner muttered.

Logan tossed Sydney a first aid bag. She caught it easily and shot a glare at Gunner. "No," she said definitely, "you can't." She sucked in a breath, then ordered, "Now take off that shirt."

Slade, Logan and Cale were all in the villa, but it was a big space, with a living area, a kitchen and two bedrooms.

Gunner stripped off his shirt, and the breath she'd just sucked in burned in her throat at the sight of his bloody shoulder. "Lie down, Gunner. Go get on the bed." She hurried to the bathroom in order to get soap and water.

When she came back, Gunner was lying tensely on the

bed. Logan and Cale had Slade in the living area, giving her some privacy to work on Gunner.

She leaned over the bed, her knee dipping into the mattress.

Gunner caught her hand. "Don't tell him," he growled.

Her eyebrows lowered. "What are you talking about?" But the tightness in her gut told her even before he said...

"Don't tell Slade about us." The words seemed so cold. Or maybe she was just cold. "He doesn't ever need to know."

He could have just slapped her. "What about what I need?"

His jaw locked. "You need *him,* right?" he gritted out. "He was the one you loved. The one you were going to marry."

She pulled her hand from him and went to work cleaning his wound. She would *not* look into his eyes. Now she was the one who didn't want to see what expression stared back at her.

"I—I don't have anything to numb the area."

"Pain doesn't matter."

Always so tough. "Why do you have to pretend you don't feel?" The words tore from her. "When we both know that you do."

"Feeling can be dangerous."

She hadn't expected that answer, and, helplessly, her gaze flew back up to his.

His dark stare was burning with emotion, with *feeling.*

"So dangerous," he whispered.

Her heart slammed into her ribs. She put her left hand on his shoulder, carefully; then she used tweezers that she'd sterilized to go into the wound. She was lucky. No, he was. The bullet hadn't fragmented. She pulled it out, wincing for him, but of course, the man made of steel didn't even flinch.

She cleaned the wound, got a better bandage and finished patching him up.

Then she kept…touching him.

Why was touching him such an addiction to her? Warm skin, hard muscles.

"Don't, Sydney." His warning.

A warning that came too late for her.

She stared at his face. At his lips. She'd heard another woman once say that Gunner had cruel lips. Tight. Hard. She'd never found them to be cruel. She'd never found him to be cruel at all. Controlled and dangerous, yes. Cruel? Not Gunner.

"Your lip is busted." She reached for another cloth, blotted the blood away. "You didn't even try to defend yourself."

Voices rose and fell from the outer room. Logan and Cale, questioning Slade.

Slade.

For months, she'd dreamed of him being found alive. Of him coming home to her. And she was glad, so glad, that he'd been rescued. She would have risked her life a dozen times to get him out of that camp.

But…

She would also risk her life a dozen times—gladly—for Gunner.

That wasn't right, was it? A woman shouldn't feel so torn between two men.

A man she'd once said she'd marry.

And a man…a man who had carried her through the darkness. A man who made her ache, even now, for *him.*

The door she'd shut banged open against the wall. "Sydney!"

Slade's voice.

"Get away from him," Slade ordered.

She blinked and realized that, yes, she was pretty much

draped over Gunner. Her hands were on him, and he—he wasn't touching her with his hands. His hands had flattened against the bed.

Slowly, she eased back and stood on her feet, deliberately positioning herself near the bed. Near Gunner.

"Did you get the bullet?" Logan asked her, voice cautious.

Sydney nodded. "He's good now."

"No, he's *not!*" Slade lunged forward, and Cale actually had to grab him and hold him back. Slade had been going forward with his hands clenched into fists and rage blazing in his eyes. "He's a bastard who deserves to suffer!"

"He just saved you," Logan said, putting his body right in front of Slade's. "Listen, I understand that you've been through hell—"

Slade's brittle laughter broke through his words. "You understand *nothing.* You hear me? *Nothing!* You think that guy over there is your friend? That you can trust him? Hell, *no,* you can't. He'll turn on you, just like he turned on me." Spittle flew from his mouth.

Gunner eased from the bed. He was shirtless but still wearing his pants and boots.

His body brushed by Sydney's as he headed toward Slade.

"Yeah, yeah, *come on!*" Slade dared him. "Fight me like a man. Take me on…and don't just leave me to rot in a jungle like you did before!"

Leave me to rot…

"He didn't!" Sydney cried out, shaking her head. "Slade, we thought you were dead! That was the only reason we left. If we'd known the truth, we would never have left you in that jungle."

His twisted grin called her words a lie. "*He* knew."

What?

Slade pulled away from Cale and pointed one shaking finger at Gunner. "That bastard, my *brother,* knew."

Sydney shook her head.

Gunner just stared back at Slade.

"It's easy enough to tell if a man's breathing or not," Slade continued. "Especially for someone with Gunner's special training."

Sydney took a step forward. "We *both* thought you were dead! We were in a firefight. You went down, and there was so much blood…"

Slade yanked open his shirt, revealed the scars on his chest. She knew those marks. Bullet wounds. "I was down, not dead." Then he looked back up at Gunner. "But you were hoping I'd die, right? Just leave me to bleed out, and that way, you never had to get your hands dirty."

This was crazy.

She met Logan's stare. Logan looked…angry? But guarded. Why? He was Gunner's friend. He knew better than to believe these accusations. They all knew better. "You're traumatized," she told Slade. "Not thinking clearly. When we get back to the States, everything will be—"

"He wanted you."

The words fell heavily into the room.

Gunner tensed. She saw the muscles of his chest and shoulders tighten.

She cleared her throat. "I—I know things are confusing for you, Slade." *Two years of hell and pain.* "But Gunner loves you. He would never have left you if he'd known—"

"He. Wanted. You."

Slade's blazing stare seemed to scorch her skin with his rage.

Sydney shook her head.

"I was in his way," Slade said. His eyes were bloodshot. Wild. "So he saw a way to take me out."

"This is crazy! We were in Peru back then to *save* you. Your plane went down. We came in to get you out! Why come in at all if we just wanted to leave you to die?" Surely he'd realize that his words didn't make sense. He'd start to understand, to see reason.

But his hands were fisting again. "*You* wanted to save me. He followed you here, because he couldn't stop you then. He was waiting for his moment, just waiting...willing to do anything to get you."

Gunner had asked her not to tell Slade about them. But Slade was acting as if—

"He got you, didn't he? I can *see* it in his eyes."

Her cheeks burned.

"Enough." Gunner's snarl.

"Not even close," Slade fired right back. "They tortured me, for *two years*. And during all those months, just how many times did you make love with my—"

Gunner lunged forward. This time, he was the one who had to be pulled back. Logan grabbed him and held on tight.

"Let him come at me! Let him take me on...instead of running away with *my* girl!"

"Stop." The quiet word broke from Sydney. Her head was throbbing. For all of the times that she'd imagined Slade's rescue, she'd never imagined *this* scenario. "Just...*stop*." Then she was marching toward Slade. "He had to drag me out of the jungle. I almost died, too. He was shot, so many times, we were both barely moving." Why couldn't he understand what had happened?

Slade glared down at her. "You moved well enough to survive."

Her chin lifted. "Search parties were sent after you. Again and again. We kept looking."

"Not hard enough."

The rage in him seemed to burn past any control.

"Get him out of here," Logan ordered, giving a jerk of his head toward Cale. "Put him in the second villa, guard him and make sure he cools down."

Cale put a hand on Slade's shoulder.

Slade immediately jerked away from him. "Don't believe me?" His voice rose. "None of you believe me? You think you can *trust* him? That I'm crazy?" He laughed again. The sound was rough and wild. "Then just…*ask him.*"

She glanced at Gunner. Logan had released him, and now Gunner stood as still as a statue. The white bandage was a stark contrast to his tanned skin.

"Ask him, Sydney. You do it," Slade urged. "Because it's all about you, right?"

"No, it isn't." The throbbing in her head was getting worse.

But Slade kept talking. This wasn't the man she remembered. So much rage. "Ask him!" Slade yelled. "Ask him if he wanted you, even then."

She stared at Gunner. His eyelashes lifted and his gaze held hers.

She couldn't bring herself to ask the question.

"Take him out," Logan ordered again.

"I saw the way you looked at her then. The way you look at her now! I was in the way!"

Cale pulled Slade toward the door.

Slade kept shouting. "You saw your chance, and you took it. You played hero to her, but you left me to die! You got just what you wanted—*her!*"

Sydney flinched.

"Tell her!" Slade was fighting against Cale's hold. "Tell her the truth. She deserves it! We both do! Look at her. Look at Sydney and tell her how you felt about her…tell her about all the times you'd watch her when you didn't think anyone saw." His voice dropped. "But I saw. I always saw."

His voice was ugly and mean and he was so far from the Slade that she'd remembered. Captivity could twist a man—or a woman—she knew that. It would take months, maybe even years of therapy before the Slade she knew returned.

If he ever did.

"I knew you wanted her, but she wanted *me!* She wasn't going to you, not while I was there. So you got me out of the way." Slade's chest heaved.

She stared at him, seeing past the long hair and beard. His nose had been broken. She could see the rough bump along its bridge. There was a long, thin scar under his right eye. Another scar bisecting his left eyebrow. And that limp...

"Tell her!"

But Gunner wasn't talking.

Cale had Slade near the entrance to the villa now, but all of a sudden, Slade stopped struggling. His cheeks were flushed dark red, his eyes glittered, but his body just froze.

Then he looked at Sydney. "Shouldn't he be defending himself?" Now his voice was flat. From screaming to flat.

Sydney shivered.

"Shouldn't he be trying to tell you that I've got it all wrong?" His voice seemed hoarse. "Why isn't he talking?"

Why wasn't she? Sydney cleared her throat. "You're confused, Slade." She tried to make her voice sound soothing. But her words broke because her control was fracturing.

"Did he wait a few months...or did he go after you right away?"

The question had her gasping. "It wasn't like that!" Gunner hadn't gone after her at all. Not for two years. Not until...

The last mission.

When she'd told him that she'd moved on.

They'd been moving on, together.

"You're wrong about him," Sydney finished, voice quiet. "You'll see that, soon."

Gunner still hadn't spoken.

"No," Slade exhaled on a low breath. "You're the one who's wrong, and *you'll* see that...soon."

Then he was leaving the villa. Cale followed on his heels. The door shut behind them with the softest of clicks.

Silence.

Sydney was still staring at that shut door. Her body was tight and aching, as if she'd just been through another vicious battle. Maybe she had.

"Gunner..." Logan's voice. "Gunner, you know it's the stress. Slade is going to have PTSD, he's going to—"

Gunner shook his head. "He meant what he said."

"Yeah, well, if he meant it, he was wrong." Logan was adamant. "I know you, and that...hell...that's not the way you operate. You don't leave a man behind, especially not your brother."

She couldn't read Gunner's expression.

"But I did leave him behind," Gunner said softly. "Isn't that why we're all here now?"

She wanted to grab him and shake him. "You tried everything you could!" If it hadn't been for Gunner, she would have died on that mission. He'd barely managed to get them both to safety.

"Rescue teams went back. They saw no sign of him." Logan's sigh was ragged. "Stop beating the hell out of yourself over this."

"You already let Slade beat the hell out of you." Sydney didn't even know why she said those words, but...

Gunner glanced at her. The darkness of his eyes was a banked heat. "Why didn't you ask me?" Soft.

Logan whistled. "Okay, I'm going to check in with Mercer. Syd, you, uh, finish up in here, and then we'll talk about our exit strategy."

Then he was gone. Pretty much rushing in his haste to get away.

Gunner rolled his shoulders, as if pushing away a painful memory. Then he stalked toward her.

She didn't move, even though she had the urge to flee.

"He told you to ask me," Gunner said. "So why didn't you?"

Because she hadn't wanted the others to hear his answer. Because some things should be between the two of them.

"You thought he was right, didn't you?"

"Not about you leaving him," she whispered. Logan was on the phone in the outer room, but still close enough that she worried he'd overhear them.

A muscle flexed in Gunner's hard jaw. "You thought I wanted you."

This was the hard part. The part that would tear her pride to shreds, but what did pride matter now? "No, but I knew I wanted you." That was her secret shame. She'd been with Slade; she'd met him first…

Then she'd met Gunner.

And in the beginning, Gunner had made her nervous. He'd put her on edge, every time that she was near him.

Slade had been the one to offer quick compliments. To take her out on fun dates.

She hadn't exactly had a whole lot of fun in her life up to that point.

Her parents had always been so strict, her dad an ex-colonel who ran a tight ship.

Then her mother had died. A sudden heart attack when Sydney was just fourteen. Her dad and his tight ship…they became lost after that. Broken. She'd had to be the caretaker, growing up too fast.

Until her father had slipped into a bottle and not come out again.

She'd been eighteen when he crashed his car.

She'd joined the air force just two weeks later.

Slade had been the Ortez brother she met first. The one with the ready smile, the big dreams.

But it had been Gunner whom she was always so intently aware of. Gunner who put her on edge with his heated stare.

She'd agreed to marry Slade, though, because she *did* love him, and he'd said that he loved her.

While Gunner…back then, he'd barely seemed to tolerate her at all.

Gunner wasn't saying a word now. Just staring at her. And she'd already said enough for them, hadn't she? "Get some rest," she told him, and turned away. She was supposed to stay in another villa, the one on the far end. Only she wouldn't be going there first.

She needed to talk to Slade. Alone.

She headed for the door. Logan had his back turned to her as he talked into his phone, but she had no doubt that he'd heard every word she said to Gunner.

"You don't have to lie." Gunner's flat words. Stopping her.

Insulting her. "Is that what you think I'm doing?" Her fingers curled around the doorknob. "Then maybe you don't know me half as well as I thought."

And she left him.

"Cale, do you mind if I speak to Slade alone?"

Cale stood in the doorway of the second villa, his broad shoulders stretching to take up the space. He stared down at her with hooded eyes. "You sure that's what you want to do? He's pretty messed up right now, Sydney."

"I need to talk to him." To find out what had happened to him. Where he'd been all that time.

Cale gave a slow nod. "Okay, but if you need me, I'll be right outside."

Her eyebrows climbed. She was EOD; she could take care of herself.

But Cale's lips curved in the ghost of a grin. "You just look so delicate…"

A lie. But she used that delicate trap to fool many of her enemies.

"Sydney?" Slade's voice sounded subdued. Good. Maybe he was calming down.

"Right outside," Cale murmured as he slipped past her and gave her the privacy that she needed.

Slade came toward her, his steps uncertain. Only fair, considering how uncertain she felt right now.

"I thought about you," Slade said as his gaze slid over her face, "so much." Then those slow steps of his were coming toward her. He wrapped his arms around her, pulled her tight against his chest.

Why did being in his arms feel wrong? Sydney forced her own arms to lift. To hug him back. "I'm glad you're alive." That was the truth.

He tensed. "At least one person is."

She eased back so that she could stare up at his face. "Gunner is glad, too. He's your brother—"

"*Half* brother."

A distinction that Slade had pointed out before, but Gunner…he never had.

"He didn't know that you were out there," Sydney whispered to him. "Search parties went back to recover you—" She'd almost said *your body.* "But no one found any sign of you." She shook her head. "Where were you, Slade?"

"I don't know." Gruff. Lost. "The first few months were

a blur." He stalked away from her, began to pace the living area. "Different camps. Shacks. They dragged me through the jungle so many times."

"And they never tried to ransom you?" Why not? It didn't make sense to her. If you've got a valuable hostage, you use that hostage.

"I wasn't the only prisoner they had. Some were ransomed." He stopped his pacing. "Some were killed."

She rocked forward onto the balls of her feet. "Are there others still being held?" If there were, they needed to get another rescue team ready.

"No. I was the last." He swung to face her. His chin shot up. "Look, I don't know why they didn't kill me, too. I don't know why they dragged me around. Sometimes I wished that they *would* kill me."

"Slade—"

"Sometimes I just wanted it all to end." His throat moved as he swallowed. "They would…they would ask me questions some days about my life—about you."

Her heart was pounding faster. When she and Gunner had been held, their captor had asked them about the EOD. "Did you tell them about Elite Ops?" Slade hadn't been in the group, but he'd once gotten clearance to work as a liaison on a mission with the group.

"Yes." Hushed.

That was how the leader had known about their division.

"I told them. I would have told them *anything* for food and water."

The mercenary who had come after EOD agents a little while back…that mercenary had been hired by someone in South America. Someone who had learned about the EOD from Slade?

No wonder his captors left him alive. They knew they could use him in order to get us.

"I want him investigated, Sydney."

There was a sharp edge in his words now. He'd seemed almost…calm…a moment before, but now Slade was marching back toward her, his limp barely noticeable. "Did you hear me?" Slade demanded. "I want Gunner investigated. He left me to die. He's not getting away with what he did to me."

She had to make Slade see reason. "We both thought you were dead. Slade, we had your funeral." It had nearly ripped her apart to stand there with the scent of flowers choking her.

But Slade laughed. "I'm sure that was exactly what he wanted."

No, it hadn't been. Gunner's eyes had been haunted at the grave site.

"I'll tear the whole EOD down if I have to do it, but Gunner won't get away with what he's done." Then he was standing right in front of her, glaring down at Sydney. "I'll make him pay, I swear I will."

His eyes looked…wild. And his hands were shaking.

"Slade, are you all right?"

"You were with him, weren't you?" Angry, low, biting.

Sydney squared her shoulders. "You've been through—" Hell. "I don't want you getting so worked up, okay?"

"Worked up?" he yelled.

She winced.

"You have no idea just how 'worked up' I can get." His smile was mean. Not the flirtatious grin that she remembered. "But you're all about to find out."

The door opened behind her. She figured it was Cale, coming back inside to check on her because he'd heard Slade's raised voice.

Slade's eyelids flickered. "Sydney, do you still love me?"

The man's moods were shifting constantly. Too fast. A

break because of his captivity? Or something more? His eyes were bloodshot, lined with deep shadows.

"Sydney?"

"Of course," she said, and it was true. "You have to know that a part of me will—"

The door closed again.

Not Cale.

She spun around, yanked open the door and saw Cale standing to the side and Gunner stalking toward the beach.

"Now he knows," Slade said, sounding satisfied, "and now it's time for *his* world to be ripped apart."

SLADE STARED OUT at the pounding surf. He couldn't remember the last time that he'd seen the ocean. The scent of the salt water was strong, and a million stars glittered down on him.

He'd shaved his beard and used a knife to cut his hair. He still didn't feel quite human, but then, he hadn't felt so for a very long time.

Sydney was gone. She'd headed back to her villa.

But not back to Gunner.

He wouldn't let her go to Gunner. His brother actually thought that he hadn't realized how Gunner felt about her. Slade had known. He'd always known.

I had something you wanted. He'd enjoyed keeping Sydney on his arm, showing Gunner what he'd never have.

His big brother, the one who was supposed to be so strong and tough and perfect.

Sydney would now see that Gunner wasn't perfect.

They'd all see.

Slade was a survivor. He was the strong one. And Gunner...

He was the one who'd be destroyed.

Chapter Five

She couldn't sleep. Sydney threw off the sheet that she'd yanked over her body, and climbed from the bed. She was wearing a pair of old jogging shorts and a T-shirt.

Sydney ran a hand through her hair. She'd been in that bed, tossing and turning, for hours. Every time she closed her eyes, she saw Gunner.

And Slade.

"It's time for his world to be ripped apart."

No, no, it wasn't time for that. Sydney hurried toward the sliding door and left her villa. She wasn't going to be able to sleep until she talked to Gunner. Things were going to be rough for them all, but they would get through this.

He'd heard her say that she loved Slade. She *did* love him, but her feelings weren't the same as they'd been two years ago. She wasn't just going to abandon Slade, but she also wasn't planning on losing Gunner.

He meant too much to her.

Her footsteps were quiet on the sand. Any sounds that she made were instantly swallowed by the pounding surf. Cale and Slade were in the second villa, Logan and Gunner in the third.

She walked past that second villa.

The moonlight shone down on her. There were no clouds

tonight. No dense jungle. Just beauty, stretching all around her and—

A sharp retort cut through the night, the sound popping like a firecracker. Sydney knew exactly what that pop was, and even as her arm burned from the bullet as it grazed her flesh, she was diving down into the sand.

Gunfire.

Had the rebel group found them? They'd put so many miles between them, switched vehicles, made a false trail.

They shouldn't have found us.

Then more gunfire came, kicking up the sand near her. She tried to hunch down, to make her way closer to the shoreline so that she'd have at least the slope of the sand to hide behind.

She hadn't even thought to bring a weapon with her. Amateur mistake. But she'd just been going to see Gunner. Taking a quick stroll had seemed safe enough.

Now she was a target.

The shots were coming from the right, from the dense shadows just past Gunner's villa. Her breath heaved in her lungs. The bullet had just grazed her. She'd been lucky.

Very, very lucky…especially considering the big target she must have made as she walked down the beach.

Then there were more shots, but not coming from the right near the last villa. Her team was rushing to help.

Cale was beside her in seconds. He crouched down, even as he kept his gun aimed at the spot where the shooter had been. "You all right?"

What was a little scratch? "Fine… Slade?" Because maybe he was the real target. Maybe the group wanted their hostage back.

"He was gone. He went out for air." His head lifted, just a bit, as he scanned the area. "Logan was going round, trying to get behind the shooter." His words were a mere whisper.

Silence. The pounding surf kept pummeling the beach. She expected to see Gunner come rushing up to join the fight.

He didn't.

After a few more minutes, Logan appeared. "Get to better cover," he ordered, and they rushed for the nearest villa.

Gunner still wasn't there. Neither was Slade. Sydney licked dry lips. "Gunner?"

Logan glanced toward the door. "He needed some time alone."

Her heart was racing too fast. "We have to find him! If he's out there, he could be in danger."

"It looks like the shooter is already gone." Grim. Only there was something about Logan's eyes, that hard, brittle glare that had Sydney on edge. "Just one shooter," Logan muttered. "Just one, and he cleared out fast."

"You think he tailed us?" Cale asked as he glanced carefully through the blinds.

Logan gave a quick shake of his head. Then his gaze fell on Sydney's arm. "He hit you."

"Barely a scratch," she whispered. "Look, we have to find Gunner and Slade!" They were the priority, not her flesh wound.

Logan's fingers curled around her good arm. "You were in the moonlight, walking on the beach?"

She knew where this was going. "Good thing he was a bad shot, huh?"

Logan didn't speak.

"Incoming," Cale murmured.

Then Gunner was there, rushing inside. "I heard gunfire!" His gaze flew to Sydney, dropped to her arm. "You're hit!"

She pulled away from Logan. "It's nothing."

Slade followed behind him, rushing in just a few seconds later. His chest was heaving. "Shots…there were shots…"

She straightened her shoulders. "I think it's safe to say that this location has been compromised."

But Logan wasn't saying that. Logan was staring at both Gunner and Slade, and she knew suspicion when she saw it.

Neither man was armed.

And Logan shouldn't be suspicious of them.

Should he?

Where were they?

Her arm throbbed.

"We're moving our departure up to *now*," Logan snapped. "I'm calling in some favors and getting us the hell out of here."

Gunner was glaring at her arm. Slade was breathing too hard, and a knot was forming in her stomach.

Because she wasn't sure…why would a lone enemy follow them? Why just take shots at her and leave?

The attack almost felt…personal.

As her blood dripped onto the floor, Sydney realized that the danger from this mission was far, far from over.

FOUR WEEKS. FOUR weeks had passed since the team had come back to the United States.

Gunner stared down at the street below him. He was in D.C., at an office most wouldn't ever know existed. He'd been called in, along with the rest of the Shadow Agents, for a briefing with the big boss himself, Bruce Mercer.

Four. Weeks.

Once they'd gotten back onto U.S. soil, Slade had been taken in by other EOD agents. He'd been sent to a hospital, examined, monitored.

And Sydney had been at his side.

His back teeth ground together.

Slade had insisted that Sydney come with him, even as his brother had yelled for Gunner to be investigated.

Locked up.

He'd tried to talk with Slade, over and over, but his brother wouldn't answer his calls. His brother wouldn't talk to him at all.

When he'd been six, he'd discovered that he had a little brother. A boy only two years younger than he'd been.

His father had never believed in commitment of any kind. Gunner's parents hadn't been married, and when his mother had contracted a deadly strain of pneumonia when he was a toddler, his father hadn't been willing to keep his son.

So his father had gone to the doorstep of Gunner's *shinali,* his Navajo grandfather, and he'd just…left Slade there. Gunner had been two years old.

For a long time, he'd thought that his father would come back.

Then he *had* come back.

But only long enough to drop off his second son.

"His mother died in childbirth. You know I can't handle kids. Let him stay here, with Gunner. They're family."

Those words still whispered through Gunner's mind, as if they'd been said just yesterday, instead of over twenty-seven years ago.

His grandfather had been an honorable man. He'd taken in the second child, and, blood or no blood, he'd loved Slade.

They'd become a family. Gunner's father had signed away custody of both his boys. Then he'd just…vanished.

Gunner had always been glad to have a brother. *I wasn't alone then.*

But as they grew older, his relationship with Slade had changed. Slade had pulled away from their grandfather.

He'd seemed to resent the small house, the sparse lifestyle that they led.

He'd seemed to resent Gunner.

And he hates me now.

The door opened behind Gunner. He looked back, too fast, thinking it might be Sydney because he knew she'd been called into the office, too.

It wasn't Sydney. Bruce Mercer stared back at him. The light glinted off Mercer's bald head, and his eyes, a dark brown, studied Gunner.

Not much was known about Mercer, if that was even the guy's real name. But the man was connected to nearly everyone in Washington, and he knew exactly where all the bodies were buried. Figuratively and literally.

"I've been told that I have to investigate you," Mercer said as he crossed the room.

Gunner stiffened. "If that's what you have to do."

"The thing is I don't *like* being told what to do." Mercer lowered himself into the leather chair at the head of the conference table. "I especially don't like being threatened."

Who would have been dumb enough to threaten that guy?

"Slade Ortez has said that if you aren't taken into custody, he'll go to the media and expose the EOD."

What. The. Hell? Slade knew that secrecy was the only way that the EOD could get their missions done. If any of the agents currently out on missions lost their covers, the results would be disastrous.

"He still knows names and faces from his time as a freelance agent." Mercer's eyes narrowed. "He gave all of that intel to his captors, you know."

Yeah, he knew.

"Now he's ready to tell anyone in the media who will listen to his story." Mercer shook his head. "I can't let that happen. You understand, right? I'll take any steps—do anything necessary—to protect my division."

Even if I get locked up?

Mercer's fingers drummed over the manila file that he'd brought into the room. "Sometimes we *think* that we know a person, but it turns out we really don't."

"Sir, I don't understand." Was Mercer saying he thought Gunner was guilty?

Mercer's head cocked as he studied Gunner. His fingers kept drumming. "What do you value most in this world?"

Sydney. Her name whispered through his mind, but he didn't speak. Couldn't.

Mercer nodded. "And just what would you be willing to do in order to protect what you value?"

Anything. Even let her go. Before he could answer, a knock sounded on the door.

Mercer held his gaze for a moment longer. Then he said, voice cool and calm, "Come in."

Sydney came in first. Gunner tried to school his expression. He'd stayed away from her, tried to give her the space that she needed. She loved Slade, so that meant he was supposed to step aside, right?

Then why did it feel so damn wrong?

Logan followed her inside the office, with Cale right at his heels.

Gunner's gaze, almost helplessly, drifted over Sydney. She looked too pale, and she seemed thinner.

His lips compressed.

"Glad you could all join me," Mercer murmured, "because it seems that we have one very big problem on our hands." His fingers had stilled over the manila file. "Just what are we going to do about Slade Ortez?"

"Do?" Sydney repeated as she crept toward the table. Since when did she creep any place? "What do you mean by that?" She waited a beat, then added, "Sir," as if she realized she was coming across too hard.

One of Mercer's dark brows rose. "You know he's threatening to go to the media."

"Every damn day," Logan muttered, taking the seat closest to Mercer. "It's getting harder to keep him in check. I thought his behavior would settle down the longer he was here, but that's not happening."

"We have to stop him." Mercer motioned for the others to take their seats. When Cale sat near Logan, Gunner had no choice but to sit near Sydney. Her scent rose up, filling his nose. So sweet. That light vanilla that haunted him.

"Just what do you have in mind?" Cale asked cautiously.

Mercer pursed his lips, but instead of answering, he flipped open the manila file. "Have any of you heard about a drug called *muerte?*"

Death. Gunner leaned forward. He made sure not to touch Sydney. "It's a black-market drug from South America." He'd heard rumors about the drug for a few months.

"One that's supposed to be highly addictive," Logan added.

Mercer studied the papers before him. "Highly addictive, and very deadly to its users. It can cause increased aggression, paranoia and even hallucinations." He glanced up at them, letting his gaze drift over the group. "The DEA believes that *muerte* first appeared in Peru, but now it's being transferred all the way up the chain to Mexico." He paused, then said "It hasn't made its way to the U.S. yet."

Gunner waited, knowing there was more to come. Mercer wouldn't be telling them about the drug unless it related to the case. To Slade.

Increased aggression. Paranoia.

"We ran a tox screen on Slade Ortez shortly after he was brought back to the States." The papers rustled in Mercer's hands. "The screen showed that he had high levels of the drug in his system. More tests indicated that he'd been using for…quite some time."

Gunner felt as if a fist had just slammed into his chest.

"You think…" Sydney's voice was hesitant. "You think his captors made him take the drug?"

Mercer's bald head tilted to the side. "They could have used it to keep him better controlled. Controlled prisoners are the easiest to handle," he said, and Gunner knew the man was talking from dark experience. Then Mercer sighed. "The way the man is making these threats, the way he's fighting every shrink I send to help him…I think the *muerte* is still affecting him."

"Can it have an impact after so long?" Cale asked. "He's been here for weeks."

"*Muerte* is one of the most dangerous drugs that the DEA has seen." Flat. "Its effects are far-reaching, and our government researchers think that some of the behavior changes can be permanent for the users."

Gunner shook his head.

But Mercer wasn't done. "Once a user's on it, it's nearly impossible to break free."

"B-but he has been free," Sydney said. Gunner saw her hands fist in her lap. "Slade's been here for weeks, and he hasn't used—"

"The shrinks say his behavior is becoming even more erratic. He needs help, the kind that he can't get without the government's help." The lines around Mercer's eyes deepened. "We have a special facility that we're going to send him to—"

"You're locking him up?" Sydney asked, voice rising.

"For his own safety."

And for the good of the EOD. Gunner understood, without Mercer having to say the words.

"I want you to convince him to go into treatment will-ingly," Mercer said as his attention focused on Sydney. "You're the one he trusts. You tell him that we can help him."

"Can you?" she fired right back.

"Maybe." A brutal answer because of its honesty. "Or he may be so far gone that there is no pulling him back."

Gunner wouldn't flinch. His brother, the kid he'd prom-ised his grandfather that he would protect…this was how he'd wound up? "Make him better," Gunner growled. "Help him to heal."

Mercer's stare shifted to him. "If I can, I will."

"And if you can't?" Sydney pressed. "What then? You can't just leave him in this—this *treatment* facility indefi-nitely—"

"If he doesn't get better, we'll explore the next step."

What would the next step be? If the behavior changes were permanent, if there was no way to stop the aggression and the threats and the—

"He's here now." Mercer was back to looking at Sydney. "I had him brought in."

Gunner knew that Mercer had actually been keeping a guard *on* Slade. Making sure that Slade didn't carry through on his threats to speak to the media.

"I want you to go and talk to him. Get him to under-stand that we aren't the enemy, Sydney." Again, another flicker of the man's gaze toward Gunner. "That *none* of us are his enemy."

Sydney rose. "I want to see that file first."

Mercer pushed it toward her. Her gaze scanned the re-ports, and Gunner heard her suck in a deep breath. "If he doesn't get treatment?"

"According to my doctors, his behavior is just becoming worse. The paranoia and aggression have only increased while he's been back in the U.S." His lips tightened. "If he doesn't get some serious intervention and treatment, he'll become a danger to himself and others."

If he wasn't already. The way Mercer was talking, the guy *already* thought Slade was a threat.

"He needs your help," Mercer said, his voice softening. "Are you going to leave him—"

Her head jerked up at that even as Gunner shot to his feet. *Low blow.*

"Or will you help him?"

Sydney's fingers were trembling as she pushed the file back toward Mercer. "I'll help him."

"Good." Mercer had obviously gotten just the outcome that he'd wanted. "He's one floor below us, second room on the right."

She headed for the door.

"Convince him, Sydney," Mercer ordered, the words heavy with an unmistakable command.

"I just want to save him," she replied. Then she was gone. The door closed quietly behind her.

Mercer's gaze swept over the agents in the room; then his stare rested on Gunner. "Make sure your brother understands the situation."

Gunner gave a jerky nod even as he headed for the door.

Once he was away from them, his steps picked up and he hurried down the hall. Sydney was already gone on the elevator, so he took the stairs, three at a time, and he was standing in front of that elevator when the doors opened.

Her eyes widened in surprise when she saw him.

Before she could speak, he caught her arm and pulled her toward him. He knew this floor well. He'd spent enough time at the EOD facility to know every inch of the place. He didn't take her to Slade—he knew Slade was in the room with the guard stationed at the door.

Instead, he took her back and to the left. To the old conference room that would be empty.

"Gunner." She started to dig in her heels. "I have to talk to him."

"You're talking to me first." He pushed her inside the conference room and secured the door shut behind him.

Then he turned around and just…stared at her. She was pale, and he didn't like that. There were a whole lot of things he didn't like just now. "What are you going to do?"

She huffed out a breath. "I'm going to get Slade help. That's what we're both going to do."

Through gritted teeth, he asked, "Are you still marrying him?"

Her eyes widened. "That's what you want to know?"

"Are you?" Because if she was, he would back away. No, damn it, his brother was hurting. His captors had strung him out on their poison. He *would* back away, no matter what. "He's the one who loves you." Gunner forced the words out.

If possible, she seemed to become even paler. "And you don't?"

His chest ached. "We had a good time, Sydney." He didn't let emotion slip into his voice. He couldn't weaken. "But he's the one you promised your forever to."

She took a step back. "A…good time?" Her voice faltered. "That's really all I was?"

No, she'd been everything, to him.

She still *was* everything to his brother. "Slade needs you," he said.

"And I'll be there for him. I'll help him." Her voice was tight. "I always planned to help him."

Then she was marching forward.

Gunner stepped out of her path.

She reached for the door, then stopped. "Did you really have to pull me aside just to tell me that you didn't love me?" The pain in her voice seemed to tear into him. "Trust me, Gunner." She glanced back at him, and he saw the sheen of tears in her eyes. "I already knew that."

She left him.

I never said I didn't love you.

He sucked a deep breath. One. Another. When his hands were steady, he left that room. A turn down the hallway showed Sydney just slipping past the guard.

Gunner's stare slid over the hall. Slade was being held in an interrogation room. That meant the area adjacent to that room would be designed for surveillance.

Gunner's steps were silent on the heavily carpeted floor. After about ten feet, he stopped, going not in the room with Slade, but into the surveillance room.

The surveillance room was dark, but he didn't bother turning on the light. Through the big wall of glass—a two-way mirror—he could see perfectly into the area next door. He could see Sydney. See Slade.

Mercer had sent him after Sydney because the boss had wanted to make sure that Slade went in for his treatment.

But Gunner knew that Slade didn't want him anywhere close by, so he'd keep his distance.

He'd just taken the first step to keeping that distance. When his brother was well—and he *would* be well; Gunner would do everything possible to make that happen—Slade would have his chance with Sydney.

After his years of captivity, Slade deserved happiness.

Gunner would make sure he got it.

"WHY THE HELL am I here?" Slade demanded as he crossed his arms over his chest. "I'm sick of this EOD crap. You hear me, Sydney? *Sick of it.*"

She swallowed and eased into the chair across from him. Mercer's words replayed in her mind. *Increased aggres-*

sion. Paranoia. Yes, she'd sure seen that with him. But how much was due to the drugs? And how much was a result of the torture that she feared might have fractured his mind?

"Slade, you need help." She kept her voice soft and easy, trying to soothe him.

He shoved out of his chair and leaped to his feet "What I *need* is to have my brother locked away, but the EOD isn't doing that." His cheeks flushed. "I gave them time. I gave you all time, and that time's run out. I'm going to the press. I'm telling them everything."

She stood, reaching for his hands. "You know the EOD's work is classified."

"I don't care." He yanked away from her.

"The man you used to be—he cared."

"That man died in a jungle.

She flinched. "I think…I think that man is still inside." She had to be very careful. "I want to help you get him back. I want to *help* you."

His eyes searched hers. "How you gonna do that?"

This was the tricky part. "Mercer has a place for you to go. The doctors there can get you well."

"You think I'm sick?" he snarled.

Yes. "I think…" She inhaled a heavy breath that seemed to chill her lungs. "I think your captors gave you something while you were down there. They made you…take some drugs, didn't they?"

He stilled.

So she kept talking. "The drugs are changing you. Making you do things, say things, that you wouldn't normally do. But we can help you—"

"You're not going to stay with me." His flat words had her floundering.

"Slade, I—"

"Whenever I touch you…" He came closer and touched her cheek.

She flinched.

"You do that," he said, and his hand dropped. "You can't *stand* for me to touch you anymore, can you?"

"Slade…" She locked her knees and refused to give in to the urge to back away from him. "You need the help—"

"I *need* you, but he's between us. Always between us."

"This isn't about Gunner!" It wasn't. "It's about getting you back to normal. Getting your life back."

"What life?" Spittle flew from his mouth. "Without you, what the hell am I supposed to do?" Then he moved quickly, faster than she'd anticipated, especially with his limp, and his hands grabbed her arms, right under her elbows. He yanked her up on her tiptoes, forcing her body close to his. "Tell me, are you going to marry me, Sydney?"

"We can't—we can't even think about that now. We have to get you well. That's the priority, that's—"

"Are you going to marry me?" He was yelling at her.

This wasn't the man she'd known. "I want him back," she said, lifting her chin. "I want the man I knew back. We're getting you help. No matter what else happens, we're getting you help."

His hold tightened. "You won't answer my damn question." His hold was so hard that she knew he would leave bruises on her arms. "Have you been with him?"

"Slade—"

"You had sex with my brother."

She flinched. *I made love with him.*

"And you won't marry me. Back in Peru, you said…you said you still loved me, but you didn't mean the words, did you? Just trying to keep me calm, controlled." He said the last word as if it were a curse.

Sydney shook her head. "That's not what I was doing! I care about you, Slade. A part of me will always love you."

He dropped her. She stumbled, almost fell when her knees wanted to wobble. Her heart was racing fast, as fast as it did when she was in combat.

Slade turned away from her. "I don't want your help, Sydney. I don't want Mercer's help. I don't want anyone's help." He strode toward the door.

She rushed after him, grabbed his arm.

Slade spun around and hit her. Sydney wasn't expecting the move, so she didn't have time to block the blow. This time, her stumble wasn't from weak knees. Then he was shoving her, slamming her against the wall. "You think you're getting away from me? You'll *never* get away from me!"

She tried to kick out at him, but he trapped her legs and—

"Let her go!" A roar. Gunner's roar. The door banged against the wall, and in the next breath, Gunner was grabbing Slade and throwing him across the room.

Sydney tried to suck in deep breaths. She'd been in fights before. She'd been on battlefields, but…but this was different. This was Slade.

Gunner.

Gunner caught her hands and tucked her gently into his side. "Are you okay, baby?"

Slade snarled.

Gunner put his body in front of hers. "You know better than to *ever* raise a hand to her. Our grandfather taught us…you never hurt a woman. You *know* that."

"That fool didn't teach me a thing!"

Sydney peered over Gunner's shoulder. Saw that the guard was holding Slade in a tight grip.

"He was a good man." Gunner's voice boiled with fury. "And you were once, too."

But Slade…laughed?

"You will be again." Now that booming voice—that came from Mercer. He'd just appeared in the doorway, right behind Slade and the guard. "We're getting you help, son."

Slade broke away from the guard and lunged for Gunner. *"I'll kill you!"* His fist flew toward Gunner's face.

But Gunner caught that fist. Caught it and shook his head. "No, you won't. And you *won't* ever hurt her again, either." He grabbed Slade, twisted his body around and held him in an unbreakable hold. "You're going in for any kind of help that the doctors can give you."

"It's a treatment facility," Mercer murmured, watching them all carefully. "For veterans. They can give you what you need."

Slade was trying to break away from Gunner. But Gunner held him in a tight grip.

The guard came forward and Mercer gave him—handcuffs?—to put on Slade. More guards entered the room, and they all started dragging Slade out.

Her heart was still racing too fast. Her hands were trembling, so she balled them into fists.

"You think you're safe with him?" Slade shouted. He wasn't going easily. Kicking, head-butting. "You don't know what he's really like!"

At that moment, she felt as if she didn't know what anyone was really like. Her jaw hurt from where he'd hit her, and her arms throbbed. Nausea rolled in her stomach, and her cheeks seemed to be going numb.

"He wanted you, so he took you!" Slade's voice was just getting louder. "He got me out of his way once, and he's doing it again now!"

"Damn it, I'm trying to get you *well!*" Gunner snapped.

"He won't let you go—he won't! If he can't have you, then he'll make sure…he'll make sure that no one else does, either! That's why he's sending me away, that's why—"

The guards pulled him through the door. Sydney kept trying to suck in some much-needed oxygen. The room was spinning on her. Why was the room spinning?

"I'll take care of him," Mercer said as he slipped away to follow the guards and the sound of Slade's yells.

Her cheeks didn't feel cold anymore. Pinpricks of heat were shooting across them.

"Sydney…" Gunner turned back to face her. His face was locked in tight, angry lines. "Did he hurt you?" His gaze locked on her jaw. "Hell, of course he did. I see the mark he left on you."

She shook her head. "I—I'm fine." The words were such a lie. Sydney took a step forward. *Don't fall apart now. Don't. Soldiers never fall apart.* That was what her dad used to tell her. *"A good soldier never falls. You carry on, no matter what."*

She took another step, trying to carry on.

But the spinning wouldn't stop. And the room got dark so fast. She tried to grab for Gunner, but then she couldn't grab anything. Her body went limp, and Sydney felt herself crashing to the floor.

She couldn't even cry out Gunner's name.

Couldn't do anything…but collapse.

"Sydney!" Gunner caught her before she hit the floor. He dived forward and wrapped his arms around her. He pulled her up into his arms, against his chest, holding her as carefully as he could. "Syd?"

Her head sagged back. Her eyes were closed.

Fear stabbed into him as he rushed for the door. "I need

help, *now!*" His bellowing voice seemed to echo down the hall.

Slade was near the elevator. He turned, and his face went slack with shock when he saw Sydney in Gunner's arms.

"What did you do?" Slade shouted.

Slade had been the one to hit her. The one to hurt her. And Gunner had never wanted to attack another man more in his life.

His brother.

And he could have ripped him apart. When he'd seen Slade punch Sydney...

"Get a medic!" Mercer barked; then he was running toward them. "What happened to her?"

The guards pulled Slade onto the elevator.

Gunner kept his tight hold on Sydney. "She passed out." She'd been trying to reach for him. There had been confusion and fear in her eyes. She'd wanted him.

He hadn't been able to get to her fast enough.

He pulled her closer, held her tighter.

Nothing could be wrong with Sydney.

As he stared down at her, desperate, Sydney's eyelashes began to flutter.

"Open your eyes," he whispered. *Please.* Because he needed to see that green gaze again. Needed to see her, without the fear in her eyes.

Slowly, her eyes opened. She stared up at him in surprised confusion. "Gun...ner? What's happening?"

The medic was running down the hallway toward them.

He wanted to kiss her, wanted to bury his face in the soft curve of her throat.

But more than that...he wanted to find out what the hell had caused her to faint. What was wrong? He had to find out, and he had to make her *better.*

Because he could take torture, betrayal, any number of

sins and punishments tossed against him, but he couldn't take anything happening to Sydney.

Not. Her.

"I DON'T FAINT." Sydney knew her words sounded angry, but *she* was angry.

And a little scared.

She was in the med room at the EOD. The doctor, a brunette with wire-framed glasses, was a woman whom Sydney actually considered a friend. So she figured she could just be blunt with Tina.

"I've been in combat zones. I've been shot. I've been under attack from all sides." She was currently sitting on an exam table. "I have *never* fainted before."

"Well, you did about twenty minutes ago." Tina offered her a small smile. "So I guess there's a first time for everything."

Sydney shook her head. "That wasn't me." She didn't want to be weak. With everything going on with Slade and Gunner, she couldn't afford any weakness.

"Sure it was." Tina lifted her clipboard. "I know you like to think you're pretty much Superwoman, but no one can be strong 24/7." Her eyebrows arched. "Not even you."

Sydney sucked in a deep breath. "I feel fine now."

"Except for that shiner on your jaw? Want to tell me how you got it?"

Slade punched me. He went crazy. He was coming to hit me again, but Gunner stopped him.

"No? Okay…" Tina drew out the word. "Then let's start focusing on what might have made you faint." She put down the clipboard. "Have you sustained any head injuries lately?"

The back of her head was throbbing now. "I hit my head when I…fell."

"You mean when Slade hit you." Crisp, without any emotion.

"If you knew, then why'd you ask?"

"Because we're friends, and I thought you might want to talk." Her fingers were carefully sifting through Sydney's hair searching for the injury. "A slight concussion could explain your fainting spell." A pause. "At least this way, I don't have to ask if you're pregnant."

Pregnant.

Sydney's heart stopped. "What?"

Tina's fingers carefully probed the bump on the back of Sydney's head. "Pregnant. You know, as in, with child? That's usually the reason most women get light-headed. It happens pretty early in term."

Sydney caught Tina's hand and pushed those probing fingers away, even as she frantically counted up the days in her mind.

"Uh, Sydney, why are you looking like that?"

She swiped her tongue across lips that were way too dry. "Can you test me here?"

Behind the lens of her glasses, Tina's eyes widened, but she quickly schooled her expression. "Of course." Then she hurried away only to return with a specimen container in her hand. But before she gave it to Sydney, she asked, quietly, "Are you okay?"

Sydney slid from the table. Took the container and didn't answer her.

Five minutes later she had the results. Was she okay? Not exactly.

Tina stared at her, waiting. A friend, not a doctor.

She was pregnant.

Chapter Six

Sydney kept a small house just outside D.C. It was about a forty-five-minute drive, but the quiet privacy she received out there was well worth the trip.

Considering all that was happening with Slade, Mercer hadn't wanted her to leave the area yet. No trip to Baton Rouge, no returning to her *real* home, not yet, anyway.

It had been three weeks since she found out about her pregnancy. Tina had done some additional testing and taken some blood samples, and she'd told Sydney that all seemed well. The changes in Sydney's body were small. Some increased sensitivity in her breasts, a little light-headedness in the mornings. Nothing too extreme so far.

And so far, only Tina knew about her condition.

She hadn't told Gunner yet, because she didn't know how he'd react.

The fact that he'd been avoiding her as if she were some kind of plague? Yes, well, that didn't exactly make telling him any easier.

Sydney sat on her porch, staring at the setting sun. The sky was red and orange, the hues stretching for as far as she could see. Her fingers were lying over her stomach. Just…there.

A baby.

Her baby.

A vehicle's engine growled, the sound too close. She tensed as her gaze darted toward the road. This was a dead-end street. Her house *was* on the end, and her only neighbors were out of town for a second honeymoon.

She wondered just who her visitor could be.

Then she saw Gunner's truck, coming slowly but steadily toward her.

Sydney didn't rise to her feet. Didn't rush out toward him, the way she had done too many times in the past. She just kept swinging, nice and casual, and soon Gunner was in her driveway. He climbed out of the truck and headed toward her porch.

As he approached, he didn't start speaking. Just stared at her with those dark eyes. What had made him come visit her? Had he finally decided that he just couldn't live without her? Because she'd had that fantasy a time or twenty in the past two weeks.

She forced her hand away from her stomach. "Gunner, I—"

"Slade's better."

Sydney blinked. "That's wonderful." She'd called for updates but hadn't learned much. The doctors had sequestered Slade during his treatment.

"They did an experimental therapy with him, to help push him through the worst of the withdrawal symptoms. Mercer says that while it won't be one hundred percent, Slade should soon be more like the man we remembered." He climbed onto the bottom porch step. The old wood squeaked beneath his boot. "He's going to have to deal with PTSD, but he can get through this, Sydney. He can be the man we knew."

She rose to her feet. "That's so good to hear." Because she was tired of seeing nightmares in which Slade came at her with fury on his face and with his fists swinging. "I hope he can find some peace."

"He wants to talk to you."

Now, that surprised her. "And what? You're his errand boy? Last I heard, he was screaming that you were the enemy."

"We're making progress on that." A pause as his gaze seemed to linger on her face. "He's out now, still under supervision from the EOD, but he's in his own apartment. He—he said you won't talk to him."

Because he'd attacked her. Because she knew this was a delicate situation, and with the news of her pregnancy, she had to do everything possible to protect her baby. "I've called and talked with Mercer and the doctors."

"But you don't want to talk to *him,* not anymore?"

She clenched her hands into fists so she wouldn't touch her stomach again. "Things have changed for me. And I already told Slade, a future for the two of us just won't be happening." It would be impossible.

"So that's it…you're walking away?" Confusion deepened the faint lines near his eyes. "I thought you were going to marry him."

Gunner actually sounded angry. Her own anger bloomed, but she choked it back. Anger couldn't be good for the baby. And the baby was what mattered. "Two years ago, I agreed to marry him." Even when she'd had her doubts. "We weren't perfect then, you know. Or maybe you don't." Her laugh held little humor. "I'll help him transition back to life here, I'll do what I can, but he attacked me. I can't be around anyone who will be a physical threat to me right now."

Even if it hadn't been the drugs, there was no future for them. She was in love with Gunner, not Slade. She was having Gunner's baby.

Gunner stood just a few feet away, and she so badly

wanted to tell him how she felt, but he seemed so wooden. Sydney found herself asking him, "Why did you want to be with me?"

His eyelashes flickered, a tiny movement. "Because you've been an obsession for me."

Obsession wasn't the same thing as love—wasn't even close.

She gathered her resolve and asked another painful question. He was here, talking to her, so she might as well take the chance while she could. "What do you want, Gunner? You came here to talk about Slade, I get that, but what do *you* want?"

"I can't have what I want."

Helpless, she stepped toward him. "How do you know?" Her voice softened because this was the chink she'd wanted to see in his armor. "How do you know you can't have it?"

She ached to touch him.

He retreated off that bottom step, moving away from her. "You're the only thing that matters to Slade. I think you're the only thing keeping him going."

She shook her head. Why did he continue making everything about Slade? "I'm talking about you. About me. Not him."

"But he's there."

She could feel him, standing between them. Would Slade always be there?

"He's getting his sanity back, and I can't take away what he wants most."

"You can't take it away?" Now her spine straightened. "I'm not some kind of prize to be given or taken away. I'm a person, and I choose my own path in this world." A path she'd wanted to take with him. "Tell your brother that I'm glad he's better, but there isn't going to be any marriage."

Not to either brother.

She'd already made arrangements to return Slade's ring, the ring she had locked away for so long. She couldn't keep it, because there was no future for them.

Sydney turned on her heel and marched back inside her house.

THE SUN HAD SET. Night had crept over the area, sealing everything in darkness.

Sydney's house sat at the end of the lane, lights still blazing in a few of her windows.

Gunner was helpless to look away from that sight.

"What the hell am I doing here?" he muttered in disgust, sitting in the shadows, watching her house.

He just hadn't been able to leave her. He'd tried. He'd driven nearly all the way back to D.C.; then he'd turned around and come back.

There had been pain in her eyes. Pain that he knew he'd caused because he wasn't giving her what she needed.

He opened the door of his truck just as her upstairs lights switched off.

Should he still go to her? Knock on the door—and do what?

Ask his brother's fiancée to be with him? Slade had just gotten back on his feet. He'd apologized for his accusations and behavior. Thin, pale, looking shaken, Slade had told him that he *would* get better.

Slade was out of the treatment facility. Mercer hadn't wanted to let him out yet, but the doctors had said that with continued rehab and counseling—therapy that he could receive as an outpatient—Slade would keep progressing. As a precaution—because Mercer was a man who believed in precautions—a guard was stationed at Slade's new apartment.

And Gunner was standing in front of Sydney's house.

Like some kind of lovesick fool. She was sleeping. They could talk later. He didn't have to—

He could smell smoke. Gunner stiffened even as he inhaled—and yes, that was the scent of fire.

The scent was coming from Sydney's house. As he turned his horrified gaze on her house, he saw the flash of flames on the bottom floor. Flames...

"Sydney!" He ran for her house, rushing up the steps and kicking in the front door. The old lock gave way easily, and he saw the flames inside, growing fast, as they raced around her living room and toward the stairs.

Toward Sydney.

"Sydney!" he yelled again even as he leaped forward. The flames were trying to lash out at him, but he jumped over them and took those stairs as fast as he could. How had the fire started? Why was it spreading so rapidly?

Where was—*"Sydney!"*

Her door swung open. She stood there, wearing a small pair of shorts and a T-shirt. She was coughing and trying to cover her mouth. "Gun...ner?"

He grabbed her. He hurried toward her bed, snatched up her covers and wrapped them around her. Then he turned back for the door.

The fire was already climbing up the stairs. Gunner hesitated. He wasn't sure if he would be fast enough to get her through the flames. They were burning so bright and hot.

He backed into her room. Slammed the door shut with his booted heel and whirled to face the window.

Sydney struggled in his arms. "Gunner, I can..." She coughed. "I can help..."

He put her on her feet. Only long enough to shove open her bedroom window and stare down below. A one-story drop. Maybe a broken leg, depending on how he landed. Could be much worse, though, if he—

"I can't go through that window." Sydney had backed away. "I can't jump!"

He caught her arms and pulled her right back against him. "You can't go down those stairs, baby. You wouldn't make it." Not without receiving burns all over her body.

There were tears in her eyes. "I *can't* take that drop, I—" Then her eyes widened. Her hands twisted in his grasp, and her short nails dug into his skin. "The storage room down the hall. There's a lattice leading down from the window there. We can go on that!"

If the lattice held them.

Sydney scrambled and jerked on a pair of sneakers

Giving a grim nod, he grabbed for the blanket and bundled her up once more.

"Gunner, stop, I can—"

He had her in his arms. If the fire was coming, it would get him first.

He rushed down the hallway, holding her tight. The rising smoke was so thick now that every step burned his lungs. He coughed hard, trying to clear his throat and chest. Not working.

Then he was at the other door. Inside that storage room. Carefully, he put her down on her feet. The window didn't want to open, as if it had been sealed shut, so Gunner just used his fist to break the glass. The glass rained down on the ground, his fingers bled, but he didn't care. He could see the lattice, just to the side. It looked old and shaky, and he sure didn't have a whole lot of faith in it.

It wasn't going to hold them both at the same time, that was for sure. But he'd already planned to get her out first.

She'd dropped the cover. It was smoldering, smoking. Sydney's glance locked on his.

"Go," he told her. "Get to safety, and I'll be right behind you."

She nodded and then she—kissed him.

He hadn't expected the move and it was all too brief. A frantic brush of her lips against his, and then Sydney was climbing through the window holding tight to that lattice.

As she climbed down, Gunner realized that he was holding his breath.

Then the lattice started to crack. He heard the wood groaning.

Hurry, Syd. Hurry.

Her feet touched down on the ground. "Come on, Gunner!"

He was already out the window. He grabbed the lattice and double-timed it, and when the wood snapped, when the lattice broke in two, he leaped the rest of the way to the ground.

No broken bones. No burns. They were both damn lucky.

He caught Sydney's hand, and they rushed away from the fire, heading toward Gunner's truck. The hungry blaze was destroying that house, burning higher and higher with every moment that passed.

If he hadn't come back, would Sydney have been able to get out on her own? He hadn't heard any alarms sounding in her house. If she'd been sleeping…

She might never have wakened.

He pulled her into his arms, held her close against his chest. His heart was racing, and fear had sent adrenaline spiking in his blood.

Too close.

He never wanted Sydney that close to death again.

THE FLAMES WERE sputtering out. Sydney stared at the charred remains of her home. Gutted. The firefighters were still using their hoses, and the scent of ash filled the air.

Sydney stood by Gunner's truck, her shoulders hunched.

The blaze had spread quickly. She'd been in bed, drifting off to sleep, when she'd heard Gunner shouting her name.

Her eyes had flown open. She'd run to her bedroom door, and only *then* had she felt the heat of the flames and smelled the smoke.

"You're sure that you had fresh batteries in your smoke detector?" The question came from Logan. As soon as he'd heard about the fire, he'd raced out to the scene. Good thing he'd still been in D.C. Logan and his new wife, Juliana, divided their time between D.C. and Juliana's beach home in Biloxi.

"Yes, I'm sure." She'd checked it a week ago. The smoke detector had been working fine then.

It had just failed her tonight.

"Good thing Gunner was here," Logan murmured. "I think he saved your life."

Again.

She nodded.

"Uh…just why *was* Gunner here?"

Her gaze slid to the right. To Gunner. He was talking to some of the firefighters and looking pretty angry.

"Sydney?"

She snapped her attention back to Logan. "He was… He came out earlier to tell me that Slade was doing better, that he was doing outpatient rehab and counseling now."

Logan nodded. "He is. I saw him at EOD headquarters just yesterday. Seems like a different man…" His words trailed away. He tilted his head to the right. "So…Gunner came out and just…decided to stay with you?"

Why was he asking her all of these questions? "No, he left. I didn't even realize he was back until—until I heard him yelling my name." Her gaze slid back to Gunner.

He was staring at her. He started to make his way toward her.

"You can ask Gunner if he saw anything or anyone before the fire started. I sure didn't see anything. I thought I was alone."

"Yet Gunner was here."

Yes, he had been. *Why?* It wasn't as if she'd stopped to ask him when they were rushing out of the burning house.

"The chief says it looks like arson. The way the burn marks are sliding across the rooms…" Gunner drew closer as he spoke. "An arson investigator will be out tomorrow to start the investigation."

"Arson?" Her hand was on her stomach. She dropped it. "Why would someone torch my house?"

"With you in it?" Gunner growled.

She flinched.

"You know the EOD has plenty of enemies." This came from Logan.

Sydney nodded. Yes, she knew that.

"You're thinking someone is targeting us again?" Gunner demanded as his stare turned to the other man.

Logan shrugged. "We never found out the identity of the man who sent out the hits before. Just that he was based in South America. We've got agents in the EOD who are digging for more intel on him even now." He paused, glanced toward the charred structure that had been Sydney's house. "This isn't random chance, we all know that. I'm going to send out word that all of our agents need to be on alert until we can learn more."

Sydney was sure that the EOD's own investigators would be joining the arson crew tomorrow.

"In the meantime, Sydney, do you want to stay with me and Juliana?" Logan asked her.

"I—"

"She can stay with me," Gunner said instantly.

That sounded like a very bad idea to her. Sydney shook

her head. "Thanks, both of you, but I'm perfectly capable of getting a hotel room. Or maybe even going back to Baton Rouge—"

"No." Gunner was adamant. "If you leave the area, you'll be on your own."

In the EOD, you were never supposed to be on your own. The other agents were there to always have your back.

The way Gunner had protected her tonight. He'd fought the flames to get her out.

Tell him. She had to tell him about the baby. Gunner had a right to know that he would be a father.

"I've got an extra room," he told her, voice stilted. "You'll have plenty of privacy."

Logan just looked between them.

She thought of her baby. She thought of the night someone had tried to shoot her on the beach in Peru. She thought of the flames that she could still feel against her skin.

If someone was after her, and it sure was starting to look that way, she wanted protection.

Gunner was the best agent she knew. "I'll stay with you," she said softly.

In the moonlight, she could see the expression of relief flicker across his face.

Just what expression would he show when she told him about the baby?

When they were alone again, she'd find out.

HE WATCHED THEM from the woods. The firefighters were still running around the scene like ants, spraying everything down with their hoses.

But no one had started to search the area.

They were too busy working on the fire.

His jaw ached, and he realized that he'd been clenching his teeth. Gunner shouldn't have been there. He'd watched

Gunner drive away before. Had *followed* Gunner out there, then waited until he had left.

It had been easy enough to sneak into Sydney's house. She'd been in the shower. She hadn't even heard him.

Not when he'd poured the gasoline all over the ground floor of her home.

Not when he'd lit the matches and started that blaze.

He'd escaped, running to his shelter in the woods to watch the flames, but then he'd seen Gunner running into the house.

Always playing the hero.

Always screwing up his plans.

So Sydney was safe now. Or so she thought. But this wasn't the end. Not even close.

He watched them. Her and Gunner. Their bodies brushed against each other as Gunner led Sydney around the truck and opened the passenger door for her.

Where would Gunner take her? Back to his place?

Bastard.

But he was going to make Gunner pay. By hurting Sydney, he'd be striking blows against Gunner.

He knew Gunner's weakness, and he was ready to use that weakness against him.

He slipped deeper into the woods. He would attack again, and the next time Gunner wouldn't be in time to ride to the rescue.

"Don't worry," Gunner told Sydney as he unlocked the door to his third-floor condo. "The EOD will find out what happened at your place."

She brushed by him as she headed inside. She was still wearing just her shorts, T-shirt and sneakers. There was ash on her cheek. Her hair was tousled. Her eyes were huge.

She was so beautiful that he ached.

Gunner squared his shoulders, then shut and bolted the door. "You'll be safe here. I promise."

"Are any of us ever really safe?" The quiet question caught him off guard. "You know as well as I do that this world is a very dangerous place." She turned away from him and paced toward the large glass window that over-looked D.C. "Safety is what we make of it."

He stared at her back, at a loss. He knew he'd do any-thing possible to keep Sydney safe, but—

"Why did you come back?"

He took a cautious step toward her. "Because there was more to say between us."

"More?" She wasn't looking at him. "Yes, you're right, there is more." Then she turned to face him. "There's some-thing that I need to tell you."

He braced himself. *There's something that I need to tell you*...usually didn't foreshadow anything good.

What was she going to say? He hoped she hadn't changed her mind and decided to go back to Baton Rouge. He knew Mercer had been pressuring her to remain in the area.

Gunner needed to stay close and keep an eye on Slade, but he couldn't just let Sydney go off on her own when someone as threatening her.

"I'm pregnant."

He hadn't heard her right. Gunner shook his head.

Sydney's lips tightened. "Don't look at me like I'm crazy. We both know you just heard what I said." She spun away. "Jerk."

He rushed toward her and spun her right back around. His hands were wrapped around her shoulders, but he kept that grip as careful as he could. "Say that again."

"Jerk?"

"Sydney—"

Her breath blew out. "I'm pregnant." Her gaze held his.

Right then, he finally understood what people meant when they said the world seemed to stop for them.

His eyes dropped to her stomach. Flat, smooth. He shook his head.

"Tina says I'm in the first trimester, and if I go back and count to when we were together in Baton Rouge—"

"I didn't use any protection." He'd been so desperate for her.

And...he knew everything about Sydney. Just as she knew everything about him. They had blood work run all the time for the EOD. They'd both been all clear in terms of health, and he'd been desperate, so desperate, that he hadn't held back long enough to protect her. "I'm sorry, I—"

"I'm a big girl, you know. I could have told you to stop. I wanted you, just the way you were." She paused, then whispered, "With nothing between us."

The woman was about to shatter his control, and he'd been trying so very hard to stay in control. For her.

"This is why you fainted," he said. *Sydney's pregnant with my baby.* The joy was there, building in his chest, but he didn't know how she felt. And—

Slade.

Slade wasn't going to handle this well.

"This is why I fainted," she agreed.

He wanted to drop his hands, to caress her stomach. Slade was going to be furious. He'd betrayed his brother, taking a risk that he should have never taken but...

My baby.

He couldn't stop the spread of joy.

"I thought you deserved to know."

The fire tonight hadn't just put her life at risk. It had put their baby's life at risk, too.

"Looks like you're going to be a father," she whispered, and she stepped back from him.

He didn't know what to say. In that heavy silence, her lips trembled and she gave a little nod. Then she was walking away, heading into the guest room. Of course, Sydney knew where his guest room was. She'd been in his condo many times over the past two years, and the place always felt better, brighter, when she was there.

"Looks like you're going to be a father." Her words rang in his ears.

In that instant, he thought of his own father—the way the guy hadn't been able to get away from him fast enough. His father had ditched him and hadn't looked back.

He'd ditched Slade, too. Gunner's grandfather had taken him in. Had raised them both, in that house with the threadbare carpet and the sagging roof. His grandfather had taught them to fish, hunt and hike.

They hadn't had much money. No fancy clothes or cars. But…

Grandfather took care of me. Loved me.

Gunner sucked in a deep breath and wondered about his own child. The child that was so small now, barely more than a dream, growing inside Sydney.

Girl? Boy? Would she have Sydney's smile? His eyes?

"Looks like you're going to be a father."

His hands were clenched into fists. He would be a father, but he would *not* be like his old man. He would not abandon his child.

Never.

SYDNEY'S EYES FLEW open as the last of the nightmare ripped through her mind. "Gunner!" His name tore from her, even though she was more asleep than awake. But she could still see the nightmare. The flames coming for her, trapping her.

And the baby.

Gunner burst into the room, flipping on the lights. He

had a gun in his hand and his body was tight with tension. "Sydney?" He searched the room, looking for a threat.

But there was no threat here.

Only a fading nightmare.

She sucked in a deep breath. What was happening to her? "Sorry. Bad dream." He'd been in the dream. He'd died trying to get her out of that fire. She'd watched him burn.

Then she'd been alone with the flames.

Her hands fisted around the covers.

Gunner took a steadying breath of his own, then carefully put the gun down on the nightstand. "Want to talk about it?"

She shook her head. "I'm fine now."

He stared at her, then gave a slow nod. "Aren't you always?"

Sydney wasn't sure what that was supposed to mean.

"I'm…sorry, for earlier," he said gruffly.

Her head tilted back. "You mean when you got all quiet and looked like you might run from the room?"

His eyes widened. "I didn't."

Okay, he hadn't fled. His face had just gotten even harder, even darker.

"You know…my father abandoned me and Slade."

Yes, she knew.

"My mother died when I was two, so it was just me and my grandfather for a long time. I used to…used to see the other kids with their dads, and I was so damn jealous."

She held her body perfectly still. Gunner didn't talk about his past much. Neither did Slade. Slade had just told her once that his childhood had been a waste, that he'd *never* go back to a life like that.

She hadn't pushed him for more. If his past was painful— if Gunner's past was painful—then she didn't want to be the one stirring up old wounds.

"Gunner, you don't have to tell me—"

"Yes, I do. You're having my baby. You deserve to know everything about me." He came toward the bed, hesitated, then sat down beside her, immediately taking up so much space and making her feel hyperaware of him.

What else was new, though? She always seemed to be hyperaware of him.

"Until I was ten, I kept hoping that one day he'd come back. That he'd realize he wanted me and Slade. That he would try to make us into a family."

Her heart ached because she could only imagine the pain he'd felt then.

"But at ten, on my birthday, when another year passed and there was no letter, no phone call, I knew it wasn't happening. He didn't care about me. He never would."

She reached for his hand and twined her fingers through his. "That's his loss."

"That's what my grandfather said." The ghost of a smile lifted his lips. "But when you're ten and your father can't be bothered to find out if you're alive or dead, it can still make you feel worthless."

"You're not—"

His fingers pulled from hers and then pressed over the covers that shielded her stomach. "I don't ever want this baby to feel the way I did."

She had to blink away tears. "She won't." She? He?

"I don't want to be like him."

"You aren't." He had to see that.

"I want to be there, in this baby's life."

Why hadn't she told him sooner? This man before her, the man whose fingers were trembling as he stroked her stomach, he wasn't a man who'd run from fatherhood. He was a man who seemed to want it almost desperately.

"I don't want the baby to feel… I don't want the baby to be like me."

He was breaking her heart. She wrapped her arms around him and pulled Gunner down onto the bed with her. She just…held him. "This baby is wanted. Loved already."

He held her tighter.

She hadn't expected this from Gunner. He'd—

He kissed her. She shouldn't kiss him back, not with everything that was going on between them, but she did.

Because she still wanted him.

The nightmare memory of his death was too strong in her mind.

So her lips parted beneath his. She tasted him as he tasted her. The kiss wasn't rough or wild, but sensual and heavy with need.

As if he were savoring her.

Her body shifted restlessly against his. She'd thought about him so many nights in the past few weeks. Every night. Wanted, and been afraid that she'd never have him close like this again.

It had just taken the little matter of fire and near death to get them together again.

He kept kissing her. He held her carefully, as if he were worried that she'd break.

She was the one to push down the boxers that he wore. She was the one to stroke his body.

He kept kissing her.

Then, still so carefully, his hands began to trail down her body. His mouth went to her neck. Licked, sucked and then he found the sensitive spot just behind her ear.…

She squeezed her eyes shut and moaned.

He tossed aside her T-shirt. Licked and kissed her breasts. The touch of his mouth on her nipples, with their increased sensitivity, had her trembling.

Sydney lifted her hips. Helped him to ditch her shorts and underwear, and then she parted her thighs.

Gunner started to thrust, but then he hesitated. "I don't—"

No, he'd better not say—

"I don't want to hurt you," he finished, voice rumbling.

She tried to smile for him. "You won't." Physically, she trusted Gunner more than she trusted any man.

With her emotions? With her heart? She wasn't sure; the pain might come again.

At that moment, she was willing to risk it.

He thrust into her. She met his rhythm eagerly, lifting up with her hips, arching against him. He filled her, stretched her perfectly, and she gasped at the heavy feel of him inside her.

Her hands curled around his shoulders. Her legs wrapped around his hips. He thrust into her, again, deeper. The rhythm swept her away, made her forget fire and fear and nightmares.

So that she knew only him and the pleasure that washed over her and made her cry out.

He held her tighter. Gave in to his own release with a growl of her name.

Then he just…held her, cradled her against his heart and kept his hand on her stomach.

Held her, and the nightmares didn't come back.

THE RINGING OF the phone woke Gunner. He could hear the peal, calling out from down the hall. Swearing, he opened his eyes. He saw Sydney, still sleeping next to him.

Beautiful Sydney.

He eased from the bed, trying not to wake her. The dawn's light spilled through the blinds. She hadn't gotten enough sleep, and in her condition, he wanted her to get all the rest that she could.

He slipped down the hallway. Found his phone. "Gunner."

Silence, then, "Are you *whispering?*"

Crap, he had been. He just hadn't wanted to wake Sydney. Gunner closed the door of his bedroom and cleared his throat. "What do you want, Logan?"

"I *want* to alert you to a security breach." His friend's voice held a tight edge now. "I just got the call from Mercer. Someone's been trying to hack in to the computer system at the EOD."

Hell. The EOD agents *were* being targeted again. The attack on Sydney's house must be the first launch.

"The thing is…our tech guys are saying that it looks like the breach came from inside."

Now, that wasn't what he'd expected. "Another agent?"

"Not sure." Static crackled over the phone. "But the person used the computer system *at* the main EOD office. Support staff, techs—they're all being investigated now. The office is under lockdown until we can figure out what's happening."

Gunner huffed out a hard breath. "What do you want me to do?"

"Stick like glue to Sydney's side. If she's the first target in this mess, there could be another attempt on her." Logan's voice hardened. "The files that were accessed? They were linked to Guerrero."

"What?" Guerrero—now a dead man—had been a Mexican arms dealer. He'd kidnapped Juliana James, the woman who had recently married Logan. When she'd been attacked, Logan had damn near gone crazy.

So how did Logan have to be feeling now?

"Someone was trying to dig into the classified documents that we have on him. That same someone…he or she was looking at Sydney's file. And yours."

Son of a—

"I'm getting a guard put on Juliana, too." Because Juliana had been instrumental in bringing down Guerrero—and because Gunner knew that Logan would never risk the woman he loved. "If someone is looking for some payback, they *aren't* getting it," Logan vowed.

No, they weren't. Gunner would make sure that no one hurt Sydney.

Not on his watch.

She was too important. The baby was too important. The life that he might just have with them—if he hadn't already screwed things up too much—*it* was too important.

SLADE ORTEZ STARED across the city. He'd chosen this apartment deliberately, though no one seemed to have realized that fact. The EOD. They thought they were so smart.

Clueless jerks.

Once upon a time, he'd wanted to be one of them. But he hadn't made the cut into the precious program. Good enough to risk his life on freelance missions, but not good enough to be brought into the fold.

Sydney had made the cut. Gunner had. Of course Gunner had.

But not Slade.

Never as good as big brother.

The EOD was paying for his apartment. Actually, Uncle Sam was paying for anything he wanted right now. After what he'd been through, they were giving him...what had they called it? *Compensation.*

There'd never be enough compensation.

He stared through the window, looking out at the city, and looking right over at the building that housed his brother.

Yes, he'd chosen this location for a reason.

To keep a watch on Gunner.

The fools at the EOD didn't realize what a threat Gunner was. They thought he was a hero. Their mistake. He'd make sure they fully realized the error of their ways.

Sydney had made a mistake, too.

She'd turned from him. Refused to go back to the way that things had been.

She should have been grateful to be with him. Of all the women—and he'd been with plenty—he'd agreed to marry her.

Sure, he'd kept a few girls on the side, the better to stop the boredom of being with just one woman, but he'd offered to marry *her*.

As payback, she'd slept with his brother.

At first, the rage had been so strong that he'd been sure it would consume him. Last night, it had come close. He'd given in to his darker urges.

But now, with the rising of the sun, he realized that there could still be hope for Sydney, if she could be made to see Gunner's true colors. Gunner would slip up, Sydney would turn from him, and Slade would be there.

It was all a matter of time.

He kept staring across at Gunner's place.

He tried not to think about the light that had flashed on in the middle of the night. He'd been watching then, too. Through his binoculars, he'd seen that light come on. The blinds had been open. He'd seen Sydney...

Gunner...

His jaw locked.

A matter of time.

Gunner would get the payback that he had coming.

Chapter Seven

"I need clothes." Sydney curled her toes into the thick carpet in Gunner's living room. "As fun as it is to keep wearing your T-shirt…" Her hands lifted the hem of his navy T-shirt. "I need to go out in public with more than just this on."

But she looked so sexy in his shirt. With her long legs stretching forever. Gunner cleared his throat. "That's, um, being covered—"

His doorbell rang. Right. That should be her clothing. Logan had told him that he'd be sending over some articles for Sydney. Gunner hurried to the door. Glanced through the peephole. Swore. Then he looked over his shoulder. "Why don't you…uh…wait in the bedroom? I'll bring the clothes to you." Because he didn't want the man on the other side of that door seeing Sydney when she looked so…

Tempting.

Sydney shook her head, threw her hands into the air and stomped off toward the bedroom.

Schooling his features, Gunner opened the door. Cale stood there, shopping bags in his hands and a pained expression on his face. "Send me out to rescue a hostage in the jungles of the Amazon," he drawled, the Texas slipping into his voice as he stepped over the threshold, "but please don't send me shopping for women's clothes ever again."

Gunner almost smiled. He *almost* smiled, would have, if he hadn't heard the returning tread of footsteps.

"Gunner," Sydney called out, "I'm going to need some shoes, too—*Cale?*"

Cale gave a low whistle. Then he choked because Gunner stepped into his path. "I, um, brought you some clothes, Sydney."

Gunner snatched the clothes from him. "Keep those eyes up," he ordered.

Cale's lips twitched. Gunner's own eyes narrowed. Cale was about to get on his—

"Relax, Gunner. I'm sure that Cale has seen a woman's legs before, plenty of times," Sydney said, a thread of humor in her voice.

But she wasn't just any woman. She was—

Mine.

Wasn't that the way he'd always thought about her?

Gunner forced himself to take a deep breath. "Eyes. Up." He gave the order once more; then he turned briskly and marched toward Sydney.

Her eyes were…twinkling. "If I didn't know better," she whispered, "I'd say you were almost jealous."

Almost? Not even close. Cale was one of those annoying pretty boys you saw in magazines. The guys who could easily wear tuxes and blend in anyplace.

Gunner knew what he looked like. A walking bad dream most days. With all the scars on him and a face that was too rough and hard, he was hardly the man women wanted to take home to meet the family.

He never had been.

"There's no need to be jealous." She took the bags from him. "Maybe you should learn to trust me." Her steps were quiet as she headed back into the bedroom to change.

He stilled. He did trust Sydney. In the field, he always

knew that she had his back. If you couldn't trust your team members on a mission, you couldn't trust anyone.

Logan, Sydney and Jasper Adams—the man whom Cale had only recently replaced in the Shadow Agents—they were like his family.

They *were* his family.

"I don't blame you for watching her walk away. That woman is a looker."

Gunner spun around.

Cale had his hands up. "Easy there, big guy. You don't have to worry about any threat from me." His lips twisted. "Not that the woman would be interested. Hell, I knew from day one that she was hung up on you." Then, softer, "Though hell if I can figure out why."

Gunner frowned at that.

"Maybe there's a charmer hidden under the grizzly bear exterior." Cale's hands dropped. "Some women go for the guys who growl."

Once more, the jerk almost made Gunner want to smile. Mostly because he'd said, *"I knew from day one that she was hung up on you."*

"How are you going to handle things with Slade?" Cale asked him, still keeping his voice low. "Because I'm going to assume that the ridiculous plan of giving her up—"

Gunner's brows climbed. Had that plan been so obvious?

"Yeah, I figured out that martyr bit earlier. Forget that. I'm going to assume that's over now?"

Sydney was pregnant. There was *no* way he'd leave her now. "I'll always be there for my brother."

"And for her?"

No one could make him leave Sydney. Last night, hell, he still couldn't believe she'd opened her arms to him last night. That she'd given him such pleasure.

Did it mean that she still cared? Just how *much* did she care?

The real question…*can I make her love me?*

"I'll stay close to Sydney," he said, trying to keep any emotion from his voice.

Cale raked his face with his gaze, considering. "That was the order, right? Logan said you were to keep her at your side, and I'm to do backup duty, watching you both." Cale's stare drifted around the condo. "This isn't the most secure place, you know. All of these windows…"

But Gunner liked the windows. After he'd been held prisoner and tortured on a mission gone bad, he'd needed to find a place that let him look out and feel free.

It was the same reason he'd helped his brother get settled in another nearby building. One that would give Slade views so that he knew he wasn't trapped.

Free.

"Just know that I've got your back, man, okay?" Cale said. "I'll be there for you and Sydney."

That was good to know. Gunner nodded.

Cale hesitated. "Logan told you about the Guerrero file?"

"Yes."

"You know…you and Sydney were on the list of EOD agents who were targeted for takedown."

Gunner rolled his shoulders. A few months back, Cale Lane hadn't been working for the EOD. In fact, the EOD had been hunting Cale. They'd thought that he was responsible for the murders of three EOD agents.

Cale was an ex-Ranger and an ex-mercenary. His psych profile had shown that he was prone to highly aggressive tendencies and that he could prove to be unstable.

Too late, they'd found out most of that profile was garbage, and then they'd realized that Cale was being set up. They'd started working together, and they'd tracked down the real killer—a man who was systematically working his way through a list of EOD agents who needed to be eliminated.

The killer had never had the chance to finish his kills. Never had the chance to take out Sydney or Gunner.

"This could be related to those attacks. Guerrero, the EOD agent hits…it could all tie together," Cale said, voice tight.

Gunner nodded. He feared, suspected, the same thing.

"If this is the case, then the EOD has one powerful enemy, one with a grudge against you and Sydney."

The bedroom door squeaked open. Gunner looked over his shoulder. Sydney was clad in jeans and a fresh shirt. She'd put on her sneakers and was coming toward them with a smile on her face.

"You haven't told her," Cale murmured.

No, not yet, he hadn't.

"Better update her on the way," Cale said, "because Logan wants us all in for a briefing in an hour."

Figured.

Sydney's smile faltered. "Gunner? What's going on?"

He exhaled slowly. He'd never sugarcoated when it came to a mission. Of the Shadow Agents, Sydney was the best at gathering intel. There was nothing that woman couldn't get a computer to tell her, so Gunner knew that Logan would want her in the office, working with the other techs to recover data and try to pick up a trail on the hacker.

So he just told her the plain truth. "The EOD may have been compromised."

Her eyes widened.

"And it looks like the breach came from the inside."

SYDNEY HURRIED OUT of Gunner's building, her steps too fast, but adrenaline was pulsing through her. First the arson at her house, and now someone had hacked into her file? Definitely a personal attack, and she wasn't about to stand by and do nothing.

She was going hunting.

"I'll follow you," Cale said as he exited the building after them. Sure enough, she saw his car waiting a few feet down the road. Cale and his cars. The man loved the classic rides. His vintage Mustang was parked at the edge of the street. Gunner's truck waited in his reserved spot. Being a special agent did have its perks, and having your vehicle close by in case of a government emergency, well, that was important.

Sydney nodded. "Thanks, Cale, I'll see you at the—"

Gunner slammed into her. Sydney's breath was knocked from her body as she tumbled toward the ground. Gunner twisted, trying to cushion her as she fell, and in that split second she just wondered…what the—

A loud *crack* sounded.

Gunfire.

She reached for her own weapon, a weapon she'd taken from Gunner's stash in the condo. Gunner had taken her down behind the truck, giving them cover behind that vehicle. As she pushed up into a crouch, his hands flew over her.

"Are you hurt?" he demanded.

Sydney gave a quick shake of her head. Not hurt, just *mad.*

Another hit? In less than twenty-four hours?

Gunner yanked out his phone. An instant later he was saying, "Logan, get a team on my street *now.* A shot was just fired." His gaze glittered as it held hers. "It came from the northwest corner, the James Fire Building. I saw the damn glint of light right before the bullet came at Sydney."

Gunner was a sharpshooter, one of the best she'd ever seen, so *of course* he'd know where that shot originated.

"Cale's clearing civilians now, and you get that team

here ASAP." He shoved the phone back into his pocket and yanked out the gun that had been holstered beneath his jacket. They'd both left the condo armed, just in case. When you knew you were being targeted, you never went anywhere without a weapon at your side.

"I want you to stay down," Gunner told her. "Stay behind this truck until backup arrives."

She knew what he was planning, and it was not going to fly with her. "While what? You race up to that building and face the shooter on your own?"

"I can't let him take any more shots! Civilians could be at risk."

The street had been nearly deserted when they came out. Just a young couple, walking down the sidewalk. Cale had gotten them clear, but what if someone else came out?

"You need cover," she told him. "I can provide it for you."

He shook his head. "You're the target, and I'm *not* letting him take another shot at you." His gaze dropped to her stomach. "Neither of you."

Her heart was racing too fast. "You can't go in alone."

Sirens were wailing. Yes, thank goodness. Someone had called the cops—could have been someone from the building, could have been Logan. Logan knew how to get the local officials to instantly jump into action.

"The cops are going to be here any second," Gunner said as he tilted his head to listen to that approaching wail. "They're going to scare the shooter off."

Because most shooters ran at the first sign of cops, except for the shooters who'd staged the attack to bring local enforcement *into* the danger zone.

In Gunner's eyes, she saw that same knowledge.

"I have to make sure no one else is at risk."

Because he was Gunner. And that was just what he did.

Sydney nodded grimly. "I won't be able to give you much cover. He's too far away."

Gunner pressed his lips to hers. "I just want you to stay safe."

Then he was gone. Damn him, he was rushing right out into the open. She lifted up, keeping as shielded as she could, and raised her gun. If she saw the glint of that weapon coming from the northwest, she *would*—

There was no glint from a weapon. And the sound of gunfire didn't break the stillness of this morning. Gunner kept to cover as much as he could as he ran toward the building.

No shots were fired.

Sydney still didn't relax her guard.

She stayed there, armed, ready to do anything necessary if she saw Gunner get threatened.

Soon the cops were pulling up and rushing toward her, rushing for the building on the northwest corner. Logan *had* already briefed them. Now it was just a matter of seeing if they could catch the shooter.

She glanced toward the building. *Gunner.*

THE JAMES FIRE Building was abandoned, due to be demolished in just a few weeks so that a new apartment complex could be built in its place. Isolated, private, it was the spot that Gunner would have picked himself if he had to take out a target on the street below.

So as he'd led Sydney to his truck, Gunner's gaze had automatically risen to that building. A reflex act. He'd scanned the windows, then seen the glint—a glint that didn't belong. He'd pushed Sydney to the ground.

Just in time.

He'd actually felt the bullet rip right past his skin.

Now he was in the building, moving quickly but quietly,

just the way his grandfather had taught him. The element of surprise was what he needed. If his prey was still inside, stupidly waiting for another shot…

I'll get you.

But then Gunner heard the thunder of footsteps. His prey was running down the stairs. If he wanted to escape, the shooter *had* to take the stairs. The electricity in that place had been cut off weeks ago, and judging from where Gunner had seen that rifle glint, the man would have been up on the tenth floor.

That was a whole lot of stairs to take. And if the man was armed with just that rifle, he wouldn't be able to aim that thing well as he ran down the stairs.

A grim smile curved Gunner's lips as he started up the stairs. No rustle of clothing, no tap of his boots, no sound at all. Higher, higher, he climbed.

Those rushing feet came closer and closer.

Then he could see the man, his legs rushing fast down the steps.

"Freeze!" Gunner roared. He wanted this man taken in alive. He wanted to know why he was targeting Sydney—or, more likely—why the guy had been *hired* to take the shot at her. Would the boss risk getting his hands dirty like this? Out in public, with a limited means of escape? Doubtful, but Gunner would make this man turn on his boss.

The footsteps didn't stop. Something heavy hit the stairs. A shot fired.

Ricocheted?

"I said *freeze!*" Gunner yelled. "Stand down! Stand—"

The man was running toward him. Gunner didn't see a rifle. The guy was sweating. His eyes were wild as he brought up his hands. Gunner saw the handgun gripped in the man's shaking fingers.

He's not going to stop. The guy was desperate to escape,

and he was about to shoot at Gunner. The man was ready to kill, in order to escape.

Gunner didn't hesitate. He pulled the trigger on his own weapon.

WHEN SHE HEARD the sound of the shots—two shots, fired closely together—Sydney started running toward the James Fire Building. Her heart was racing fast, adrenaline burning in her blood, and she *had* to get to Gunner.

Cops were in front of her. Slowing her down. She wanted to shove them aside—so she did. Then she headed into the building with her gun up, ready to do anything she had to do in order to help Gunner.

She found him on the stairs crouched over a body.

Sydney didn't lower her weapon. Her gaze swept over Gunner. *No blood. No blood. No blood.* The mantra repeated in her head until she could breathe normally again.

"He wouldn't drop his weapon." Gunner's voice. Flat. She lifted her left hand, curled it over his shoulder.

The cops were there, fanning around the body. Gunner's shot had been lethal, right to the heart.

The man's eyes were closed. His body lay sprawled and twisted on the stairs.

"There's a rifle, sir," one of the cops said.

Sydney lifted her head. She saw the young, uniformed cop pointing up the stairs.

Gunner rose. "He ditched it when he came down the stairs. I heard him toss it. Then he…he pulled his backup weapon."

Gunner hadn't been given a choice. She understood, just as she understood that it was never easy to take a life.

Whether Gunner was following mission orders and taking out a threat through his scope or fighting an up close enemy, it wasn't easy.

Never easy.

"Gunner?" she whispered, wanting him to look at her.

His head turned toward her. His eyelashes flickered. She knew Gunner wouldn't show emotion here. She'd seen him do this before. He shut down after a kill. Withdrew.

That was the way Gunner worked.

"I wanted to take him in alive," Gunner said softly. "I wanted to find out *why,* to find out who'd sent him."

Because Gunner must think this was a hired killer, just like the mercenary who'd targeted the EOD agents before. She glanced back at the man. Early thirties, blond hair slicked with sweat. She didn't recognize his face, had never seen him before.

The EOD would find out everything they could about him. They'd run down his fingerprints. Analyze the scene.

Her gaze flickered over him. There was a tattoo on the inside of the man's wrist. A striking snake. They'd track that tattoo, too. They'd find out who this man was and why he'd been shooting at them.

Gunner still held his gun in his right hand. Sydney tucked her own gun into the waistband of her jeans, then she reached for his weapon. "It's over now."

But Gunner shook his head. "No, I'm afraid it's just getting started."

THERE WAS SO much blood on his hands. Gunner knew he'd never be able to wash all of that blood away.

He was in the EOD office. He'd been questioned, cleared, briefed. The cops had handed their investigation over to federal agents—FBI personnel who would report their findings back to the EOD.

"Gunner?"

He turned to see Sydney standing in the doorway behind him. There was worry on her delicate features.

"Are you okay?" Sydney wanted to know.

He wasn't the one with a bullet in his heart. He should have tried for a nonfatal shot, but the man had been aiming his own weapon right at Gunner's head. There hadn't been time to do anything but fire. "I just killed our lead."

She frowned, then shut the door. Then she was coming closer to him. "You just saved my life, that's what you did."

He didn't speak.

"Why do you have such a hard time," she asked him, tilting her head back to better study him, "ever seeing yourself as a hero?"

"I do my job, Syd. That doesn't make me a hero."

"It does to me." She reached for his hands. The ones that had killed so easily before and, he knew, would again. He'd always been good at killing. "When I look at you, I see the man who saved my life today. The man who has saved me dozens of times in the field. You've saved so many. So *don't*—" now an order snapped in her words "—ever see yourself as anything less, understand me?"

She stared up at him, her bright eyes telling him that he was good. That he was worth something.

The woman was going to tear him apart.

A knock sounded at the door then. Sydney still held his hands. She didn't let go.

When the door opened and Slade stood there, Gunner wished she'd let go. He saw the flash of pain in Slade's eyes, but his brother quickly schooled his expression.

"I heard what happened." Slade's color was better. Not the pale mask of death that he'd looked like when he first came back to the U.S. "I wanted to make sure you were both okay."

Slade had been given clearance to come into the EOD office. Mercer wanted private updates with him, so Slade had access to some of the floors there.

Gunner carefully studied his brother. Did he know this man now? Had he really known him before? "I'm okay."

Slade's lips twisted. "Of course you are. Killing has always been easy for you." Slade's words uncomfortably echoed Gunner's own thoughts. "Aim and fire..." He laughed lightly. "Bet the guy never even saw you coming."

Gunner stiffened.

"Killing isn't easy for anyone," Sydney said, voice stilted. "A life is a life."

"Yeah, but some trash just needs to be taken out every now and then, right? And this bozo who targeted you..." His gaze focused on Sydney's face. "I'm glad he's gone. I don't—I don't want you in danger."

Sydney pulled away from Gunner. Actually, she put her body between Gunner and Slade. Gunner was struck by the fact that...she'd always been between him and his brother. From the first moment he'd seen her and—wanted his brother's girl.

She's not his any longer.

"You heard about the fire, too?" Sydney asked.

Slade nodded grimly. "What can I do? I want to help." He waited a beat, stepped forward, then added, "I *need* to help."

"We're not sure what's happening yet," Sydney told him, voice cautious. "Slade, we don't want you putting yourself in danger. You just got out of the veterans' facility. You need to recover more. You need—"

"I need to get my life back." The faint lines near his mouth deepened. "I'm not the kind of guy to sit on the sidelines. After two years, I *need* to get back in action. I want to be normal again. I want to be me." His voice roughed. "Let me help, both of you. I want to help."

Gunner could see the struggle on his brother's face, but he also didn't want to put Slade back in harm's way. Slade wasn't in shape to handle any dangerous missions, no way.

Slade straightened his shoulders. "I can help here, okay? In the EOD office. I can do grunt work, I can read through files. I can do *something*."

"Maybe you can," Gunner agreed, because he didn't want to hurt his brother's pride. Hadn't he already done enough to him? "We'll talk to Mercer and see what can happen."

"Good." Relief flashed in Slade's eyes, then his gaze dipped to Sydney once more. "I'm so sorry." A rasp had entered his voice. "Sorrier than I can ever say. I never, ever should have hit you."

She stared back at him. "You weren't yourself." Her words were flat.

"No, no, I wasn't." He came closer to her, caught her hands.

This time, Gunner was the one to tense.

"I'll prove to you that I'm better," Slade whispered. "I will."

Then he seemed to realize that he was holding her hands. He blinked, shook his head and backed away. "I'll go find Mercer. I want to talk to him first, plead my case, you know?"

He could try. Gunner wasn't sure that Mercer would allow the guy to do much, not with all the secure intel in the facility. But Gunner would talk to Mercer, too, and see if there was something very low-risk that Slade could do, something to help make Slade feel as though he was helping them.

Slade hurried out of the room. Gunner saw that Sydney had tilted her head, and her gaze was still on the door, even though Slade was gone.

Was she realizing that the man she'd known *was* fighting to return? It was too late for going back now, too late for them both.

"Sydney…" He exhaled slowly. "About Slade—"

She turned toward him. "Did you ever find out why Slade didn't make the EOD team?"

He blinked. That was the last question he'd expected from her.

"He seems to want to be here so badly, but he told me… he told me that he withdrew his agent application."

"That's what he told me, too."

A furrow had appeared between her eyes. "That's when he started taking all those charter trips. He said he was trying to save up extra money for the marriage."

The marriage.

"But after he disappeared, there was no money in his bank account."

He knew that. He'd helped Sydney pay for the funeral. But he didn't like where she was going with these questions. "What are you thinking?"

She bit her lower lip, then shook her head. The smile she gave him didn't reach her eyes. "Nothing. I'm just worrying over nothing." She backed up a step. "The techs are waiting for me."

"Don't leave the building without me," he told her, his worry breaking through.

Sydney gave him a little salute. "Wouldn't dream of it, sir."

Then she was gone, and he was left with a faint suspicion swirling in his own mind. At the time, he'd wondered why Slade's bank accounts had been cleared out. Cleared so that only dollars remained, when Slade had been doing charters for almost a year.

His money had vanished.

Gunner had pushed aside the mystery two years ago, but now he was wondering…just where had all of that cash gone?

SLADE TOOK A deep breath, then knocked on the door that led to Bruce Mercer's office. Well, the outer office, anyway. Because when he opened the door, he saw the hard stare of Mercer's assistant, Judith Rogers. Judith looked barely twenty-five, but he'd learned that the woman had the tenacity of a bulldog. He'd tried to get to Mercer before, and she'd blocked him more than once.

When she saw him, her auburn brows rose. "Do you have an appointment?" Judith demanded.

Great. He barely managed to keep his expression polite. Judith annoyed the hell out of him. "No, but he's going to want to see me."

"I doubt it." Crisp. "Mr. Mercer is a very busy man."

"Yeah, well, I think Mr. Mercer would like to know if he has a killer in his midst, don't you?" He tossed that out deliberately, knowing that Judith wouldn't be able to ignore those words. "Of course, if you just want to stand back and let an agent die…"

She stood instantly, all five foot nothing of her. Then she pointed at him. "Stay here." Her high heels clicked as she headed for Mercer's door. She was inside for—he counted—two minutes, and then she came back and told him, "Go in, he's waiting for you."

He didn't let his grin break free. He was good at controlling his expression. At showing only what he wanted folks to see. People were so easily fooled.

So easily.

He entered the main office and closed the door. He made sure to hesitate as if he were uncertain.

You're going down, Gunner. His brother had been downstairs, with his hands all over Sydney.

Right in front of me.

"Slade." Mercer sat behind his big, fancy desk. One of

his eyebrows had climbed. "Ms. Rogers told me that you had some information to give me."

Slade glanced over his shoulder, as if he were trying to make sure that no one could hear him. Then he nodded quickly.

"Have a seat." Mercer waved his hand toward the chair in front of him.

Slade limped toward the seat, making sure to drag his leg a bit, conscious of Mercer's assessing gaze as it fell on him.

"You're looking better."

"I am better." He'd been fine all along. That rehab had been a *joke*. He blew out a hard breath. "I heard about the attacks on Sydney."

"Did you." But the words weren't really a question.

Again, he nodded quickly. "I want to help." He let his hands tightly curl over the armrests on his chair. "Give me a job to do, give me *something*."

Mercer shook his head. "There's no way you're going into the field. You have no security clearance any longer—or the training needed—for a job like that." The man wasn't pulling punches. "And physically, mentally, you're far from ready for any mission."

That's what you think. But he didn't let the rage slip out. "Give me a job here. I heard the techs talking—they think someone tried to break into the system. I can watch surveillance video, I can read files, I can do *something*."

Mercer just stared back at him. "I thought you were here to talk to me about one of my agents being a threat."

Slade flinched.

"Do you have intel to provide to me?"

Slade looked down at the floor. "I want to help so I can prove it's *not* him."

Silence.

He forced himself to look up and, sure enough, Mercer

was still watching him with that too-assessing gaze. "Give me a name," Mercer ordered.

"He didn't leave me to die." Slade forced the words out in a rush. "I was wrong. It was the drugs talking. He couldn't have left me to die."

Mercer leaned forward. "You're talking about Gunner?"

"Yes." A rasp. "He didn't leave me to die, and he didn't try to hurt Sydney."

"Why does it sound like you're attempting to convince yourself of that?"

Slade glanced at the floor, took a deep breath, then looked back up at Mercer. "Because when we were teenagers, there was this…this girl that Gunner liked. Sarah Bell. Sweet little Sarah Bell." He could still see her in his mind. "She kind of looked like Sydney. Same light blond hair, same green eyes."

"Why are you telling me this story?" Mercer snapped.

He jerked to attention. "Sarah Bell…she broke up with Gunner. Said he was too rough for her, too wild. Then a week later, Sarah died."

He could still see all the flowers that had been at her funeral. Sarah had been particularly fond of roses. He'd put a dozen on her grave.

"Her whole family died," he whispered. "A fire broke out in their house while they were asleep. Someone had disabled their smoke detector, then poured gasoline all over the first level of their home. The fire started and they…" He swallowed the lump in his throat. "The newspapers said that the family never had a chance. They didn't wake up at all."

"Did the police find the arsonist?"

He shook his head.

"And you think that relates to this case because…?"

Did he have to draw the guy a damn map? "Because Sarah was with Gunner, and she left him. He told me, he *told* me that he wasn't going to let her go. She was his, and no one would ever take her from him." His breath rasped out. "Now he thinks that Sydney is his..." He let the sentence trail away.

Silence. The kind that stretched too long; then, finally, Mercer said, "I thought you said you wanted to prove it's not Gunner. Sounds to me like you're making a case for the arsonist *being* him."

"No, I—" He raked a hand over his face. "Maybe the drugs are still in my system. I'm being paranoid. I mean... the fires aren't even the same M.O., right? I'm sure the fire at Sydney's house wasn't set by gasoline and the detectors weren't disabled—"

"None of the alarms went off at Sydney's house, and while the arson investigation is ongoing, preliminary indications are that gasoline was the accelerant used."

He sagged in the chair. "But Gunner got her out? He was the hero last night, right? Not the bad guy. *Not* the arsonist."

Mercer's gaze gave nothing away.

"It can't be him," Slade whispered.

"If you're so sure that it's not him, then why are you in my office? Why did you tell Ms. Rogers that you had intel to give me?"

His hands dug deeper into the armrests. "Because... what if it *is* him? Our father...did Gunner tell you that he wound up in a mental ward? That's where he died. He'd gone crazy, and attacked his latest girlfriend—tried to kill her." His voice sounded hollow to his own ears. "We never saw him much growing up, but Gunner and I both always wondered...just how much like him were we?" He held Mercer's gaze. "How much?"

Chapter Eight

Sydney stared at the computer screen before her, absolutely sure that there had to be some kind of mistake.

For six hours, she'd been working with the other techs. They'd gone back through the system, tracking their hacker. Gone through every system link they could find.

They'd narrowed down the security breach. It had happened three days ago, at 0300 hours. Long before anyone *should* have been in the office.

The Guerrero case file had been accessed, her personnel file had been accessed and Gunner's file had been accessed. But according to the results she was seeing, their hacker had looked at Gunner's file for only two seconds. That wasn't long enough to learn any details. Just long enough to lead a cyber trail for them to follow. Long enough to show that someone had pulled the file.

Pulled it, but not scanned any information?

If their hacker wanted intel on Gunner, why not look longer? The hacker had been given access to her file for three minutes. He'd viewed all the Guerrero files for five minutes.

And it wasn't that the hacker had been interrupted. According to the report she was generating, he'd viewed Gunner's file first.

"Why?" Sydney whispered as she stared at the screen. He hadn't gotten any data from Gunner's file, so he'd gone there to what…lead a false trail? Gunner wasn't the target, just her?

"Sydney, we found the pass code that was used to get into the system," Hal West told her as he slid his chair toward hers. Hal was the lead systems administrator for the EOD.

She glanced up at him. A pass code would be needed to open the system, but their hacker had put a virus in place after he'd gotten access, and that pass code signature had been all but erased.

All but…

"It's an old code, one that was initiated over two years ago." Hal's face looked strained. Considering that she knew the guy had been working the computers for most of the night—while she'd been escaping from the blaze—that strain was to be expected. "The agent we originally assigned the code to was given a new access number a year ago." He shook his head. "Someone screwed up. When he got a new code, all privileges associated with the previous access should have been revoked. Someone didn't terminate the code authorization and—"

"Hal!" she snapped out. "Which agent had that code?"

"Uh…right," he said as his bleary blue gaze cut away from her and back to the nearby computer monitor. "Gunner Ortez."

She shook her head, an instinctive denial. "Gunner wasn't here when the files were accessed." She didn't even know why she said the words. Just—*not Gunner.*

But Hal was tapping on his keyboard and nodding. "He wasn't, or at least, the system says he didn't gain entry until 0500, but…that's his code."

"Then someone has access to our archived codes. We need a complete wipe on the system. Even if you *think* those codes are clear, we're purging them." Her heart was beating faster. It could be a setup. She'd sure seen setups before. Poor Cale. Evidence had been planted left and right to frame him. She knew better than to jump hungrily at the first bone that was tossed her way.

But maybe their hacker didn't know about the case with Cale. Maybe he didn't realize the lesson that all of the Shadow Agents had learned then.

And maybe he didn't fully realize...*we don't turn on our own.*

She hunched her shoulders and started tapping on her keyboard. This was an inside job, she didn't doubt that, but it wasn't Gunner. It wasn't Logan. It wasn't Cale. She trusted the other Shadow Agents with her life.

But she wouldn't overlook any possibility. Logan had assigned her to gather intel, so she would. She'd start by going back through the personnel and access files of every agent and support staff member who'd entered the EOD in the past six months.

She wasn't going to stop until she found more than just a red flag. She'd find hard evidence.

GUNNER STARED AT the charred remains of Sydney's house. Only a shell remained, blackened, gutted. When he thought of Sydney in that fire, fear knifed into him.

"Good thing you were here."

He glanced over to see Logan heading toward him. When Gunner had arrived moments before, Logan had been talking to the arson investigators.

Gunner remembered the brush of the fire on his skin as he ran up the stairs. "Yeah. Very good thing." If he hadn't been there...

"They actually found one of her smoke detectors. Fried, warped, but..." Logan glanced toward the house. "They managed to pry it open. The battery was missing."

What?

"It's definitely arson, of course. The chief says the point of origin was downstairs—actually, he says there were three points of origin. The guy wanted to make sure the house burned fast."

"He wanted to kill Sydney." Gunner's rage darkened the world for a moment.

From the corner of his eye, he saw Logan give a grim nod. "Yes, he did. The perp used gasoline as the accelerant. Disabled the alarms, waited until she went to bed…" He glanced over his shoulder at the woods that lined her property. "Probably waited out here, watching her, and when he thought he had the perfect moment to attack, he went to work."

The SOB.

"Why were you out here?" Logan's question was quiet, tense. "I mean, you and Sydney seemed to be staying away from each other at first, and now—"

I won't stay away from her again. He'd only come out there to do some on-site investigating. She was nestled inside the EOD office. With all the agents there, with Cale pulling extra guard duty, she should be safe.

Gunner rolled his shoulders, trying to push some of the tension from his body. "I came last night because Slade wanted to talk to her. I came out here to try to convince her to go see him."

Logan's eyebrows climbed. "You think that's a good idea?" He turned to fully face Gunner. "It's just you and me, man. So cut the bull. I've *seen* the way you watch her. What are you thinking? That you'll just step aside so he can have a shot with her again?"

Had he thought that? Or had he just felt so much guilt that he'd wanted to make amends? *I didn't know he was alive.* But for two years, Slade had suffered. Two years.

"You've been a captive, too, Gunner. The things they did

to you…" Logan shook his head. "Most men never would have come back from that."

Logan had seen him, after he'd crawled from that jungle. With his body stitched everywhere, looking like Frankenstein's monster.

"You've been through your own hell," Logan continued. "Don't you think you deserve some happiness, too?"

His hands clenched. "I wanted Sydney to have what—who—she wanted."

"And you think that's your brother? Uh, you might want to check that again. You're the one she's always watching. The way you watch her? With that too-intent gaze? Buddy, she watches you with the same stare."

"She's pregnant." The words slipped from him. Not deliberate, or, maybe they were. Because he wanted to tell someone. He had to share the news with someone, and Logan had always been a good friend.

Logan's eyes widened. "Yours?"

The question had him clenching his fingers into fists and taking a step forward. Maybe *not* such a friend for long.

Logan's hands flew up. "Of course it's yours! I meant, hell, I'm just stunned, okay? A baby… You and Sydney." He shook his head, and a broad smile split his lips. "That baby is going to wrap you around her finger!"

Yes, he was pretty sure that she would.

"A baby," Logan whispered, and his eyes widened. He glanced back at the house. "Oh, hell, man, you probably felt like your whole world was burning down last night."

"It was." Gunner didn't tell him that he hadn't known about the baby then. When he'd looked up and seen the flames, and known that Sydney was inside, yes, it had felt just as if his world was burning. Because it had been.

"We're gonna find him," Logan promised. "You know we will. With our resources…"

The EOD's resources were limitless. But even the EOD couldn't fight Mother Nature.

"A storm's coming in," Gunner said as his gaze rose to the thickening clouds above them. "That could wash away a lot of evidence." His gaze focused on the line of trees. If the guy had been out there, waiting, he might have left tracks behind. Gunner was very, very good at following tracks. "I'm going to see what I can find."

Logan nodded. "I kept the techs back because I figured you'd want first shot. Didn't want them messing up the scene."

Logan knew exactly how he liked to work.

"You lead the way," Logan continued, "and they'll be there to back you up." Then Logan clapped him on the shoulder. "Congratulations, man, you're going to make a great dad to that lucky kid."

Gunner tensed. "I...hope so."

Logan frowned at him. Before Logan could say more, Gunner headed toward the trees. He'd already scouted the area before, looking for the perfect vantage point that the attacker would have used. A spot that would provide him with good cover, but one that wouldn't put him too far away from the scene. The arsonist would have needed to get to the house quickly, and then be able to rush back and hide when the flames blazed.

Gunner wondered how long the man had stayed there. Had he watched as Gunner ran inside?

He eased through the light covering of brush at the edge of the woods. He made sure not to snap any branches. He didn't want to create any evidence confusion. His grandfather had taught him and Slade how to slip in and out of any place, without leaving any traces behind.

So far, he wasn't finding any evidence. No footprints

on the ground. No broken leaves or branches. The attacker had been careful.

But if he'd been watching for any length of time, he would have needed to find one spot. One perfect spot to sit and wait and watch. No matter how careful the man had been when he got in the woods, he would have left a sign at his waiting spot. Turned-down grass. A cigarette butt. Something. Most folks couldn't just wait for a long time in total stillness.

Gunner could. Most couldn't.

When they'd practiced with their grandfather, going out past the reservation and into the woods that surrounded the land there, Slade had always hated standing still. He'd taken to grabbing a piece of pine straw and braiding the pieces together, over and over, because Slade had needed something to keep his hands busy.

Some watchers smoked to help pass the time. A bad idea, because the prey could catch the scent of cigarettes in the air.

Some chewed gum. Some carried a toothpick.

Slade had twined the straw around his hand, an absent gesture, as he waited—and told Gunner what a stupid idea it was to follow their grandfather into the woods.

Gunner stilled and glanced back toward the house. This was the spot he would have chosen if he wanted to watch Sydney's home—to watch and not be seen. If he crouched lower, he'd be totally covered by the trees before him, but if he wanted to see, then he just shifted a bit to the left.

He had a perfect view of what had been Sydney's upstairs window.

He glanced down at the grass around him. It had bent, just a bit, enough to tell him that his instincts were right. The watcher had been here.

Gunner swept the ground with his gaze, looking for some

kind of path. He'd been on the road last night, and there hadn't been any other car on this dead-end street. That meant the watcher had stashed his vehicle some other place. Gunner knew that a highway waited, about four miles back through the woods. The guy would have needed to make a route back to that highway.

Gunner just had to find it.

The watcher was good. Gunner would give him that. It took him fifteen minutes of searching before he found the first broken branch. Sure, that branch could have been broken by a wild animal, but...

There was another snapped branch about ten feet away. Then another three feet.

The man had been in a rush to leave.

It was next to that snapped branch that Gunner stopped, frowning. He bent and picked up the braided pine straw that had been left behind.

He stared down at the straw, not wanting to believe what he was seeing. This threading...

He knew this threading.

When they'd been younger, Slade had tossed away pieces of straw like this dozens of times. His brother had twisted the straw, twined it around his hand, and—

"Gunner!"

He stiffened at Logan's call and his fingers tightened around the braided pine straw.

"Did you find anything?" Logan was closing in.

Gunner lowered his hand, squared his shoulders and turned to face the other man.

GUNNER FOUND SYDNEY typing frantically on the keyboard, her fingers flying. Her shoulders were hunched forward, and the light from the computer's monitor clearly showed the scowl on her face.

Even though the door was open, he rapped lightly. Hal, the admin working right beside Sydney, glanced over at him. When he saw Gunner, the guy's eyes doubled in size. "A-Agent Ortez."

"Hal, can I have a minute alone with Sydney?"

Hal jumped to his feet. "Sure thing." He gave Gunner a very wide berth as he hurried from the room.

Sydney just shook her head and kept typing.

Gunner frowned thoughtfully after the other man. "What's with him?"

"You intimidate him," Sydney said as she kept typing. "The way you intimidate most people you meet." She exhaled and finally pushed away from the computer and her chair spun so she could face him. She stared at him, giving him a considering look. "I think it's the eyes. The way they say, 'Yes, I've looked into hell a few times.'"

He blinked at her.

She smiled at him. "But I'm rather fond of your eyes."

No way were his cheeks flushing right now. Okay, perhaps they were, and he was very grateful for the olive skin that had to hide most of that flush.

Then her smile slipped away. "What did you find out at my house?"

He wasn't real eager to start sharing that, so he said, "What have you found out here?"

"Here?" Her lips tightened. "Here I've found out that it looks like someone used your old access code to gain entrance into the system."

"Mine?"

"Yes. Your personnel file was accessed, too, but only for a few seconds, not nearly as long as my file and the Guerrero file were."

His muscles locked. "Someone's setting me up."

She nodded. "That would be my thought." She pushed

out of the chair and closed the distance between them. "Now tell me what *you* found at my house." Pain flickered in her eyes. "Was anything left?"

"No, Syd, I'm sorry."

Her chin lifted, the way it always did when she was trying to pull her strength together. "That place...it was my retreat while I was in D.C. My *home* has always been in Baton Rouge. I'll get over this," she said with a firm nod. "I will."

He believed her, but there was still more to tell. "I tracked through the woods, looking for a sign of the arsonist."

"And?"

"I might have a lead."

She sighed. "Don't play this game. Tell me what you've got or I'll just go straight to Logan."

"I think it could be Slade." Harsh words. Words that he hadn't wanted to say, but she needed to be aware of the danger that could be right beside them both.

Her eyes widened. Not doubling in size as Hal's had, but still showing her surprise. "What?"

This was where he got to tell her that a few pieces of straw were making him suspect his brother. Flimsy evidence that hadn't exactly convinced Logan. "He was trained to leave no trail, just like I was. He's good, but..."

"Not as good as you," she finished quietly.

"He could never just sit still. He always had to do something to keep his hands occupied. He'd take pine straw, twist it, braid it." Gunner almost thought of the twisted straw as his brother's signature. Whenever they'd been kids, and he'd found the straw in the woods, he'd known that Slade had been there. "I found some of that braided straw in the woods near your house."

"But he had a guard on him. You told me—"

"Logan's checking with the guard to make sure that Slade didn't slip away." Once Logan had questioned the guard, then they'd have a better idea of where they stood. Right now Gunner just had a dark suspicion boiling in his gut.

"You really think Slade would try to kill me?"

Slade *had* attacked her once. The sight of the bruising on her jaw had enraged him. If Slade thought that Gunner was taking Sydney away from him, well, Gunner wasn't sure just how his brother would react.

The man he'd been years before…*no,* that guy wouldn't do something like this. But the guy who'd came out of the jungle, addicted to *muerte,* he just might.

"What about the man who took the shot at me? Do you think he's somehow linked to Slade? To the hacking?"

"I don't know." All he had were his instincts, screaming at him. "There isn't enough evidence yet to know what's happening." And the fact that she was turning up evidence to implicate him? That was even worse for the situation. "I just want you on guard. I don't want you ever alone with him."

She stared up at him. "My personnel file…whoever accessed it knows about the pregnancy."

The pregnancy could have been enough to push Slade over the edge. Gunner could see Slade hacking in to Sydney's file, wanting to learn everything about her, but there was no reason for Slade to hack in to the Guerrero file, *if* he even knew how to hack. "When was that access code of mine used last?"

"It's one that went obsolete—or should have gone obsolete—over two years ago."

When Slade had still been around.

The phone on Gunner's hip vibrated, right at the same time that Sydney's vibrated, too. Gunner pulled out his phone and read the text. "Tina?" he asked Sydney, sure she'd just gotten the same message from the doctor.

Sydney gave a nod, then quickly signed off on the computer, securing the machine.

Tina's text had said that she had blood test results that she needed to share with them, ASAP. She wanted them in the med room.

He knew that she'd been assisting with the autopsy on the man he'd shot at the James Fire Building. Tina didn't normally handle autopsies, but Mercer had ordered her in on this one because he wanted one of his close staff members with eyes in that morgue. And when Mercer gave an order, few folks ever refused.

Sydney was silent as they entered the elevator. Gunner felt too conscious of her every move. He wanted to talk to her about last night, but since he'd just dropped the bombshell of his suspicions on her, he wasn't quite sure how to lead into that.

He wasn't the guy with the smooth lines and easy conversation. He never had been. He actually found it hard to talk to people outside of his team. The rest of the world just didn't seem to understand him.

Especially women.

When he'd been a teen, there had been one girl he liked, a little blonde with green eyes. But when she'd talked to him, he'd pretty much wound up replying in monosyllables, and she'd started to date his brother instead.

What had her name been? He wasn't sure.

The elevator dinged. The doors slid open. Sydney walked out, and Gunner realized he hadn't said a word to her that whole time. Smooth. Gritting his teeth, he followed her into the med room.

Tina was waiting there with Mercer. Mercer had his arms crossed over his chest as he leaned back against a filing cabinet.

"Dr. Jamison has found some interesting results for us,"

Mercer murmured. Gunner noticed that the man's assessing stare drifted to him, then returned to Tina.

"It's the blood work." Tina pushed a report toward him and Sydney. "I found *muerte* in the man's system."

Muerte. "The same drug my brother was on?" His gaze snapped to Mercer. "I thought you said the drug hadn't made it to the U.S."

"That's what the DEA told me. Looks like they could be wrong about that."

Sydney whistled as she studied the reports. "These are some extremely high levels. We're lucky he didn't shoot up the whole block."

"The whole block wasn't his target," Mercer said quietly. "You were."

Sydney's fingers tightened around the report. "Do we know who he is?"

Tina nodded. "I got a hit on his fingerprints. Ken Bridges. He's ex-army, dishonorably discharged for conduct unbecoming." She cleared her throat. "He, um, almost beat a man to death while he was on a recon mission. The man was a civilian, completely unrelated to the mission."

"What had Ken been doing since the army?" Gunner asked.

"Looks like whatever he could get paid to do."

A gun for hire. Figured.

"The DEA's getting pulled in on this one," Mercer said. "They're going to investigate Ken, break apart his life and follow the trail they find back to the *muerte*."

The *muerte* trail already led to Slade. So he had to ask, "Are you questioning my brother?"

"Any intel that Slade can provide to us about the men who held him and addicted him will be used by the DEA."

Gunner gave a hard shake of his head. "That's not what I'm asking." He'd been blunt with Sydney and with Logan.

He'd be no less with Mercer. "Are you going to interrogate him? To see if he's linked to this guy?"

Mercer's head tilted as he studied Gunner. "Your brother has been either under guard or in a rehab facility for the majority of his time in the U.S. How is he supposed to have hooked up with a hired gun?"

"This guy's ex-army, right? Maybe he hooked up with him *in* rehab. Maybe there was someone there who gave him Bridges's number. If Bridges was addicted, then he'd probably know guys in that same rehab unit." It made sense. Mercer had to see that.

"If there's a link between them," Sydney said, "we can find it."

He had no doubt.

Tina was staring at them all with wide eyes.

"You think your brother is doing this? You really think he could be the one targeting Sydney?" Mercer asked as he uncrossed his arms.

"I don't want to suspect him."

"Why not?" Mercer asked softly. "He sure suspects you."

That was the last thing Gunner had expected to hear. He snapped to attention. "Sir?"

But Mercer was pointing toward the door. "Let's finish the rest of this conversation upstairs, Gunner. Dr. Jamison, good work. Sydney—"

"I want to be a part of that upstairs conversation," she said, voice tensing with a demand.

The ghost of a smile curved Mercer's thin lips. In his mid-fifties, Mercer still had the tough edge of a man half his age. "Since it's your life, I rather suspected you'd request just that."

Then Mercer walked toward the door.

Gunner glanced at Sydney, wondering what the hell she

had to be thinking about this turn of events. His brother thought he was the killer?

And I think it's him.

But the real question was...who did Sydney trust? Which brother did she think was there to protect her, and which was there to kill her?

Chapter Nine

They didn't go to Mercer's office. They went into an interrogation room, and that fact put Sydney on edge.

She glanced toward the two-way mirror. Was someone
watching them? What in the world was going on?

As far as she was concerned, there was no way that
Gunner was a suspect, and Mercer had better stop treat-
ing him that way.

"Gunner, you understand that I have to explore every
avenue in this case." No emotion broke through Mercer's
words. "You've been a fine agent here, and I have nothing
but respect for the work that you've done."

Sydney couldn't stand it. "So why are we in *interrogation?*"

Mercer glanced over at her. He and Gunner were both
seated. She was pacing like mad. "Because procedure has
to be followed, and I don't want this situation coming back
to bite me later," Mercer told her quietly.

She stopped pacing.

"So let's get through this as quickly as we can." Mercer
looked back at Gunner. "Do you know a woman named
Sarah Bell?"

Sydney frowned. The name meant nothing to her.

"Sarah." Gunner seemed to be testing the name. Then
he nodded. "I knew her, a long time ago."

The door opened then, and Mercer's assistant, Judith, hurried into the room. She handed Mercer a file. "Thank you," he told her, inclining his head.

As Judith left, Sydney was pretty sure the other woman flashed her a look of pity. Of pity? What was up with that?

"How long ago?" Mercer asked.

"I was eighteen. She was…I think sixteen at the time? Sarah Bell…she was killed in a fire."

"Yes, she was."

Mercer opened the file and pushed some grainy black-and-white photographs toward Gunner. "I pulled the arson reports on her fire. The M.O. that the arsonist used, it's the same as the one that was used at Sydney's place."

Sydney grabbed the nearest chair and sat down—hard. Then she strained to see those photographs. The charred remains of the house had her swallowing a few times. Then she saw the newspaper reports that had been printed off and included in that manila file.

Family Perishes in Blaze.

"Sarah Bell and her parents all died in the fire," Mercer said. "Unfortunately, the arsonist was never apprehended."

Gunner leaned forward. "You think I had something to do with this?"

"Your grandfather passed away a week before that fire. His passing…when he was the only one to ever provide stability to your life…it had to leave you feeling lost."

"I wasn't lost." Flat. "I had my brother to take care of. He needed me."

"He needed you, but you *wanted* Sarah Bell?"

Now another picture was pushed forward. This one appeared to have been taken from a yearbook. A young girl with curly blond hair and sparkling green eyes. In the picture, she smiled, flashing dimples.

"I never dated Sarah Bell."

"Are you sure about that?" Mercer pressed. "Because your brother said you were sweet on her back then."

Gunner started to respond, then stopped.

The tension in the room ratcheted up. *He had cared for Sarah.*

"She was a nice girl," he said. "She never seemed to care that my clothes were old or that I had to work two jobs around my school schedule. Sarah…she was good to everyone."

"I heard she wasn't so good to you."

"That's what Slade said?" Gunner asked. Sydney saw a muscle flex along his jaw.

A nod from Mercer. "He said she rejected you, and you didn't handle that rejection so well."

Gunner laughed then, but the sound made goose bumps rise on Sydney's arms. "Slade was the one who dated her, not me."

"How'd that make you feel?" Mercer's gaze bored into him. "Angry? Enraged? A girl who should be with you… but she wound up with your brother."

Gunner shook his head.

But Mercer wasn't done. "Then it happened again, didn't it? Another girl you wanted…" He cast a fast glance toward Sydney. "But she wound up with your brother."

Enough.

Sydney jumped to her feet. The chair slammed back behind her, and it hit the floor. "Stop accusing him, okay? Gunner didn't do this!"

"But his access code was used." Mercer's voice was still without emotion. "Hal told me what he discovered today."

"He discovered a setup, *that's* what he discovered," Sydney snapped. "You can't actually believe that Gunner could be responsible for this—"

"I have to explore all possibilities," Mercer said again. "Every avenue."

Sydney huffed out an angry breath. "Why would he access the Guerrero file? He has no reason to do that."

"*He's* not the one talking right now," Mercer pointed out.

For an instant, Sydney was tempted to go across that table, boss or no boss. He wasn't just going to sit there and accuse Gunner. Not while she—

Gunner's fingers wrapped around her wrist. "Easy."

He must have realized just how close she was to lunging. But the last thing Sydney was feeling was *easy* at that moment.

"Pull up your security cameras," Gunner told Mercer. She wondered how he could sound so calm. "You'll see I wasn't even at the facility during the time of the breach."

"Funny thing about that…the cameras weren't working then." Mercer's lips thinned. "This facility is supposedly one of the most secure locations in the world, and our damn security cameras blacked out. You know what that tells me? It says we were hit by a professional, one with covert skills that would let him get in and out of a building without being noticed." His fingers drummed on the table. "It also tells me that we're definitely looking at an inside job. Someone knew all of our weaknesses. Someone studied them. And that person or persons exploited them."

Sydney frowned. Hal hadn't mentioned that the security cameras stopped working during the breach. He was the one who should've had an uplink to those videos. If they went off-line, he should have been alerted immediately. "Did you question Hal?"

Mercer nodded. "Who do you think I talked to first? The man was shaking so hard he could barely answer any of my questions."

And he'd been so nervous when Gunner came into the

room. She'd just written off that nervousness because Gunner truly did make most people tense up, but what if it had been more?

Hal was the one who'd found the evidence linking Gunner to the hacking.

Hal was the one who *should* have been alerted to the camera failure.

"If anyone knew how to get past the security system," she whispered, "it would be Hal."

Mercer shook his head. "His key card wasn't used for entry that night. Hal wasn't here—"

Sydney laughed, but the sound held no humor. She was still standing and definitely didn't feel like sitting. "Hal knows the system in this building from the inside out. If he wanted to slip in, he could."

Was she throwing Hal under the bus? At this point, Sydney wasn't sure. She just knew…Gunner hadn't done this. "I want to look at Hal's computer."

Or rather the roomful of computers that he actually had.

"Sydney…" Mercer began.

"I want to check his data. He said the authorization code linked back to Gunner. Well, that code should have been deleted years ago. By Hal. I want to see his computers. I want to find out just what searches he used to find that intel." Her heart was beating too fast, but Gunner didn't seem to be defending himself. *Why not?* So someone had to prove his innocence.

She wasn't wrong about Gunner. She wouldn't be wrong. There was no way that he'd tried to kill her.

No way.

Mercer was studying her with his hard gaze. Sydney held her breath, waiting, then… His head inclined toward her. "Go search the computers."

Yes. She nearly ran for the door. This was what she

needed. What she had to do. Gunner was clear. Or he would be, once she was done.

Because she wouldn't lose faith in the one man who'd pulled her from the darkness. He'd helped her before. She'd help him now.

SILENCE FILLED THE room after the door shut behind Sydney.

Gunner knew his body was too tense, but he wasn't exactly in the mood to relax.

"She has a lot of faith in you," Mercer finally said, voice considering.

Yes, she did. Enough faith to humble him.

"You didn't seem to have as much faith in her."

Gunner's eyes narrowed.

"I mean, you were so sure that she'd go back to Slade, right? You were the one who backed away."

"Listening to gossip, are you?"

"I listen to everything. In this business, you have to." Mercer sighed. "I don't like this."

"You think I do?"

"I think you're barely holding on to your control. You're so worried about Sydney that you can't even think straight." Mercer stabbed a finger toward him. "Get your head in the game, Gunner. Stop letting your emotions rule you."

He'd never let emotions rule him. Not until—

Sydney.

"If the evidence against you keeps piling up, I'll have to act."

Those words sounded like a warning.

"My gut tells me you're clear. I *know* you, and I don't want to be wrong about you."

"You aren't." Neither was Sydney.

"Then find my perp. Bring me evidence that I can use to nail him to the wall."

Gunner unclenched his jaw. "I want Cale Lane reassigned. Get him to start guarding Slade."

He trusted Cale. No way would Slade slip by him.

"Already done," Mercer murmured. Then he rose. The legs of his chair slid back with a screech. "Protect her."

With his life.

"Sydney reminds me…" Mercer began, but then his words trailed away. Sadness flickered in his eyes, and the lines on his face deepened. The man looked as though he was skirting sixty, but Gunner had no idea at all what Mercer's personal life was like. Did he have a wife? A family?

Mercer cleared his throat. "She reminds me of a woman I knew a long time ago. I lost her."

"I'm sorry."

"You'll be sorrier if you lose her, trust me." Then he headed from the door. "There are some things that even soldiers can't recover from."

If he lost Sydney, the baby…no, he'd never recover.

Good thing he wasn't planning on losing them.

SYDNEY SWIPED HER key card over the access panel, and when the lights flashed green, she pushed her way inside Hal's inner sanctum. The Hub, as he called it.

Hal wasn't there. Good. He should have gone home an hour ago. Time for her to get working and see exactly what was happening with his system.

She eased into his chair, started typing and immediately, the screen froze on her.

Hal had installed extra protection on his machine.

Good for him. Except…she'd been there when he'd installed that protection. He hadn't even bothered to glance over his shoulder to see if she was watching while he typed in his code.

She'd been watching.

And she *never* forgot a code.

Her fingers tapped quickly over the keyboard. She knew how to get around this system. Hal never gave her enough credit.

Then she was pulling up the searches he'd used in the mainframe, and yes, sure enough, the access code had linked to Gunner. Damn it.

But she kept searching. Looking for the security video feed from the night of the breach—a feed that should have been there.

Her eyes narrowed on the screen as she read the system file for the time of 0300 on the date of the breach. There were no reported errors with the monitoring system. No reported errors at all because…

Her fingers typed faster.

Because Hal had shut off the system thirty minutes before. She could see the override, right there on the screen. He *was* in on—

"I figured you would be the one to come and look at the security logs." The door behind her closed with a soft *click*.

Sydney tensed. She'd been so intent on the monitor that she hadn't even realized that Hal had come into the room.

But as she looked up into the monitor, she could see his reflection. He was walking toward her, and he had a weapon in his hand.

A gun.

He wouldn't have gotten past the security check-in downstairs with that weapon. But they had a weapons room on the second floor. As if it would have been hard for Hal to help himself to some equipment. After all, he controlled the access to most of the rooms in that building.

She inhaled a steadying breath. She didn't have a gun, but that didn't mean she was defenseless. She was the one trained for combat. Not Hal and his nervous hands. He might think that he had the advantage, but he'd soon realize the error of his ways.

"You were supposed to die, though," Hal said. "So it wasn't going to matter. The shooter was going to take you out. You'd be dead, so you wouldn't come in here and find out about me."

"Why?" She turned and looked at him. A deliberate move on her part. For someone like Hal, someone not used to doling out death, looking into the face of his victim would be hard.

Staring into her eyes, then killing her...even harder.

Her fingers curled around the pen she'd taken from his desk.

"I didn't want to," Hal whispered, and sure enough, his hands were shaking. "I didn't have a choice. He was going to hurt my family." His eyes teared. "They're all I have... he *knew* things about them. Too much. I had to do it."

"You had to turn off the cameras?" She wanted to keep him talking. Needed to.

Hal nodded.

"And you gave him the access code?"

"Y-yes."

The shaking of that gun was making her nervous. Her body was tense, ready to attack, and she planned to lunge at him soon, but she had to time her move just right. The last thing she wanted was a bullet hitting her or the baby.

The baby.

"Do you know I'm pregnant?" she whispered. "Please, Hal, don't hurt the baby." She meant that plea. The baby—the one she hadn't even felt moving inside her yet—mattered more than anything to her.

Hal hesitated. "Baby?" The gun began to lower.

It was the moment she needed. Sydney leaped out of her chair. With one hand, she grabbed Hal's right wrist—

his right hand still clasped the gun—and she shoved that wrist out wide, making sure he wouldn't have a shot at her. Then, with her other hand, she brought up her pen, aiming for his now exposed inner arm. She drove the pen into his arm because she knew that his reflex action at that attack would be to drop the weapon.

The gun hit the floor. Just as she'd anticipated. But it discharged on impact, and the shot echoed around her.

Instantly she could hear the scream of alarms. No way would a gunshot be missed in a place like this.

Then, as Hal was howling, she brought up her elbow and slammed it into his nose. She heard the snap and saw the spurt of blood from his nose. Hal backed away from her, crouching and...crying?

Sydney kicked the gun across the room. It skittered toward the entrance. She kept her hands loose at her sides, ready to attack again if necessary.

But Hal wasn't putting up much of a fight. He was trying to stop the blood that was flowing from his nose and saying—

"I'm sorry, I'm sorry, I'm sorry..."

"You're sorry?" Sydney demanded. The alarm was hurting her ears. "You pulled a gun on me. You leaked classified information. You need to be a whole lot more than just sorry."

He stood, or tried to stand, but his body kept trembling. His hand went to his side.

Over his shoulder, she caught the movement of the door as it opened.

"I want a name," Sydney demanded through gritted teeth. "I want a full description of the guy. I want to know exactly who paid you off."

Hal shook his head. "I—I can't—"

"Do you know what happens to people found guilty of

treason? Do you have any idea just how long you'll be in jail?" Not to mention the slew of other charges that would be coming against him.

He shook his head again harder this time. "I can't… can't go to jail."

Maybe you should have thought about that before you sold out the EOD and me.

"Give me a name. If you cooperate, then—"

"I *can't!*" And his left hand came up. His fingers were wrapped around a box cutter. He had been a busy man. "*Muerte,* I—"

A shot rang out.

Sydney was staring right into Hal's gaze, and she saw his eyes widen in shock. Then his body was crumpling as he fell to the floor. She rushed toward him. *No, no, no!* He couldn't die. He knew the identity of the man who'd infiltrated the EOD.

She put her hands on either side of his head, tried to make him look at her. "Hal?"

His eyes were wide open with shock and pain.

She moved closer, forcing him to see her. "Hal, give me a name."

"S-sorry…"

"Don't be sorry." There wasn't time for sorry. "Help me, Hal. Make this right. Give me a name."

But Hal wasn't going to give her anything. As she stared at him, all of the life vanished from his eyes.

"Hal?"

He was gone.

"Sydney?"

She looked up. Slade stood just a few feet away, a gun in his hand. Hal's gun. The gun she'd kicked across the room so Hal couldn't use it again.

"I—I saw him coming at you, I thought he had a knife...."

The box cutter could have done as much damage as a knife, but she would have been able to knock it out of Hal's hand. She knew plenty of techniques to disarm him.

"I couldn't let him hurt you," Slade whispered. His eyes—filled with horror—were on Hal's still body. "I just reacted. I just...shot."

Footsteps pounded in the hallway. She could hear them through the open door. Then Gunner was there, bursting into the room. "Sydney!"

He saw Slade with the gun. He lunged for his brother.

"Gunner!" Sydney called out.

Slade didn't fight him. Gunner yanked the gun away from Slade and shoved the smaller man up against the nearest wall. Then Gunner turned that gun on his brother. "What the hell are you doing?"

Sydney rose. "Saving me."

Mercer was there, too, breath heaving from his lungs. She saw Cale and a few other agents.

All too late to change what had happened.

She straightened her shoulders. "Hal attacked me. Slade came in and...he thought he was saving me."

Gunner glanced back at her. His eyes widened as his gaze swept over her. He put the gun down on a table, and then he was across the room in an instant, his hands running over her arms. "Is the blood yours?" There was a tight, desperate quality in his words that she'd never heard before.

Sydney shook her head. "All Hal's."

Gunner's hand was resting over her stomach now.

"I'm *okay.*" They both were. She looked to the right. Mercer had crouched next to Hal, but the others were watching her and Gunner. Silent, tense.

Gunner locked his jaw, gave a grim nod and slowly dropped his hand.

She heard a ragged gasp and her gaze met Slade's. He'd seen Gunner's hand on her stomach. Seen the fear and worry on Gunner's face.

He knows.

Slade's head tilted down. His hands clenched into fists.

Tears stung her eyes. Things should never have been this twisted.

"Why the hell did Hal go after you?" Cale asked.

"Because I knew what he'd done. I found it…" She pointed toward the computer. "Hal's the one who turned off the security feed. Probably so we wouldn't realize that he was the one here that night, doing the hacking. He used Gunner's old code. Hal set him up."

Mercer's fingers were on Hal's neck, looking for a pulse. He wasn't going to find one.

He must have realized that same fact because Mercer swore and glanced up at her. "Did he tell you *why?*"

Mercer wasn't the kind of man to take kindly to betrayals. But then, who was? Only with Mercer, she knew the retribution for betraying him usually involved death or imprisonment.

"He said…he said he didn't have a choice. That his family was threatened." But if she looked into his bank accounts, would she discover that he'd been paid off? Not just threats, but an enticing wad of cash to help him escape from the EOD and start fresh somewhere else?

There was always a price that had to be paid for a betrayal.

"*Muerte,*" she whispered.

Cale's gaze cut to Slade. Slade shook his head.

"That was the last thing Hal said to me."

"Maybe he was afraid of death," one of the other agents muttered.

No, she didn't think he'd been talking about death so much as the drug. With the drug showing up in the shooter's blood, with that being the last word that Hal had spoken, the dots were connecting in a very deadly way.

"It's in the U.S." Mercer stood. He had blood on his fancy suit. "The bastards have it here, and the DEA doesn't even realize it." He waved his hands. "I want this room clear. Don't touch anything, hear me? I'm getting a crime scene analysis team sent in from the FBI. They owe me, and the feds are about to start paying up."

Sydney eased toward Slade. He looked up at her, his face pale.

"I heard the gunshot," he whispered. "I was in the hallway. I didn't…I didn't even know you were the one in here. The door was ajar…I just slipped in."

And he'd seen her and Hal in a standoff.

"When I saw the weapon in his hand…" Slade swallowed. "I just fired. I killed him."

Gunner was at her back. Silent.

Slade's gaze dropped to her stomach. He swallowed. "There… Is there something you want to tell me?"

No, she couldn't tell him. Not now. Not in front of all the others. But Slade had just killed to protect her, so she had to say something. "Thank you," she whispered, and wrapped her arms around him, giving him a hug.

His hands closed around her. She felt the light touch of his lips on her head. "I'd never let anything happen to you."

She pulled back, stared into his eyes.

"Never."

She took a step away from him.

"Slade…" Gunner began.

Slade flinched. "I know I'm about to get busted for firing a weapon in here, okay? Mercer's going to rip into me—"

"You were here when I wasn't. I just…" Gunner leveled his stare at the other man. "I'm thankful."

But there was an edge in Gunner's voice. One that gave her pause. Maybe because…

She didn't quite believe what he was saying.

There wasn't any more time for talking or questions then. As Mercer herded them out, he separated her from the rest of the group and led her to his office.

She knew her own interrogation was about to begin.

She'd wanted to prove that Gunner was innocent, but she hadn't wanted anyone to die.

Two deaths in the past twenty-four hours.

What would happen next? Because Sydney was sure the nightmare wasn't over. Not by a long shot.

SHE WAS PREGNANT.

Slade walked down the hallway, trying to keep his movements slow and easy, even as rage built inside him.

Sydney was pregnant. He'd seen the way Gunner touched her stomach, heard his brother's desperate whisper.

Cale was walking behind him doing guard duty. Slade had just saved Sydney, been the hero, and they were still guarding him.

Gunner had looked as though he would choke when he realized Slade had been the one to save the day.

Too late this time, brother. For once, someone else got to be the hero.

Cale's hand wrapped around Slade's shoulder. "Mercer wants to talk to you."

Of course he did. Mercer would want to grill him some more when he should want to pin a medal on his chest.

But Gunner was the one with the medals, and he...he was the one left to rot.

Slade nodded. "Right," he said timidly. He thought the tremble in his voice was a good touch. Made him look as if he was still shaken after the shooting.

He'd planned to kill Hal that day, one way or another. He'd known the guy was a weak link, and he'd intended to eliminate him at the first opportunity. Only he'd wanted Hal's death to be linked to Gunner. More evidence and suspicion mounted on big brother.

No matter. At least Sydney was back to thinking he was the good guy. He could definitely manage to use that to his advantage.

As for putting more suspicion on Gunner? Well, he already knew exactly what he'd do on that score. And after the next attack, Sydney would be convinced that her lover was trying to kill her.

Chapter Ten

"Sydney!" She turned at Gunner's call. She'd been heading for the elevator. It was far past midnight, and she just needed to crash.

"Are you ready to leave?" he asked her.

More than ready. She'd been heading upstairs to find him, but now they could just head out to the parking garage together.

"I had your car brought in," he told her as they slid into the elevator.

"Thanks." She knew her smile had to be tired.

Gunner frowned at her, and then he leaned forward and pressed the emergency stop button on the elevator's control panel.

"Uh, Gunner?" The elevator had stopped.

He pulled her into his arms, kissed her. The kiss was wild, hot, desperate.

His hands were tight around her, his body so hard and strong. He kissed her as if she were some kind of lifeline for him. As if he needed her to survive.

Only fair, since she needed him so very badly.

Gunner lifted his mouth a few inches from hers and growled, "I thought you'd been shot. I thought Slade had shot *you*."

But no, Slade had been the one to save her.

"There was blood on you…"

She'd switched into some backup clothes that she kept at the EOD. Those bloodstained clothes had caused nausea to roll in her belly.

"I think you scared a good ten years off my life." His arms were still around her.

Sydney stared up at him. "I didn't think anything scared you." Gunner was the tough guy. The one who could stare death in the face and never back down.

"That was before you." He kissed her again. Still as desperate. "I need you to be safe."

She needed him to be safe, too.

His gaze searched hers; then he slowly eased back. "Better get us moving," he murmured, "or Mercer will send out a search team."

Because security was on full alert at the EOD office.

She gave him another smile and waited as the elevator resumed moving.

Gunner's fingers—broad, warm—curled around her shoulders, and he began to massage her as they headed down to the parking garage.

Heaven.

But that paradise came to an end all too soon. The elevator's doors opened. The garage was well lit, with security cameras positioned every few feet. She saw her little car waiting right next to Gunner's truck.

"You can ride with me," Gunner said. "I had your car brought in, just like you asked, but there's no need for—"

"I want to take my car," Sydney said, cutting through his words. "With everything that's happening, I want to make sure that I can stay mobile on my own." If she had to clear out quickly, she wanted the security of knowing that her own ride was waiting for her.

Gunner's jaw locked, and she knew he didn't like her

answer. "I will be right behind you," he told her. "I'll follow you back to our place." He caught her hand, pressed a kiss to her fingers. "Be careful."

Our place. No, it wasn't, not yet. But maybe they could talk about their place soon. About starting a home for the family they would have.

Sydney tried a faint smile for him. "I'm a federal agent. I can do careful, no problem."

He didn't smile back. The worry was there, shadowing his gaze.

She slipped into the car. Gunner closed the driver's-side door and watched her through the window.

He hadn't talked about marriage. Hadn't really talked about their future at all other than to say he wanted to be there for the child.

Did Gunner want a future with her?

She cranked the ignition. He kept watching her as she eased away from the parking spot; then he turned and headed for his truck.

She wanted a future with him. Baseball games and barbecues and Christmases spent around a tree. She wanted to wake up next to Gunner every day, and go to sleep next to him each night.

If only he wanted the same thing.

Her phone rang, surprising her. She had it hooked in to her car's system so she just had to press one button on her console to connect with the phone system. Frowning, she took the call. "Sydney."

"Where are you?" Slade's voice. Rasping.

Frowning, she drove toward the guard booth. She saw Myles, the night shift guard, and she flashed her ID at him. He nodded, then typed in the code to raise the gate.

"I'm…uh…just leaving the office," she said. Hadn't Slade gone home hours ago?

"Sydney, *be careful*."

Her fingers tightened around the wheel. "What's going on?" She began to ease away from the nondescript EOD building.

"Don't trust him. I know you think you can, but…*don't*."

Gunner. She swallowed. "Slade, why are you saying these things?"

"Because I saw the way he was with her."

Her? Did he mean Sarah Bell?

"You don't really know him. Not like I do."

"I—I thought you and Gunner were getting along—"

His rough laugh cut across her words. "Keep your enemies close…" he murmured.

She glanced in her rearview mirror. Saw Gunner's truck following her. The flash of his headlights lit up her car.

"Gunner isn't your enemy."

"He's yours."

Her foot pressed down on the brake as she slowed to a stop. The intersection was clear, so she started to accelerate again. "Gunner isn't my enemy." He was many things, but not that. Never that.

"You're blinded by him, just as she was." He sounded sad now. "Can't you see him for what he is? I don't want him to hurt you."

"He won't!"

"He was afraid that you'd go back to me. He's trying to play the hero—"

His words cut out on her. Bad connection. "I can't hear—"

"Maybe he didn't want you to die in the fire. Maybe he wanted to save you" —static crackled across his words— "so you'd be grateful. Then he took out the shooter before he could talk. Gunner got you out of the way *before* the bullet fired—"

She was straining to hear his words.

She lifted her foot to brake as she came up on a curve.

"—he knew the bullet was coming. Playing hero again."

Her jaw locked. "Gunner isn't playing anything. Look, I can't talk now. It's late and—"

Her brakes weren't working.

The car wasn't slowing as it headed into that curve.

Sydney pushed down on the brake again.

Nothing.

She held tight to the wheel and took the curve. She came out with the vehicle pushing too fast. There was another intersection up ahead. A red light shining. She pumped her brakes, trying to get them to work. "I can't stop."

"What? Of course you can stop trusting him, you can—"

No. She pumped again. The brake wasn't working. The pedal was going all the way down to the floor and doing nothing. The light was still red for her. Other cars were whizzing right through the intersection. She was going down a hill. Faster, faster. "*I can't stop!* The brakes aren't working!"

The red light flashed to green. Her breath rushed out and her car flew through the intersection. But she had to stop soon. She had to find a place to stop.

Another red light loomed ahead.

Change.

Change.

"Sydney!" Slade's frantic voice.

The light wasn't changing.

Another car was going through the intersection.

She spun the wheel hard to the right. The passenger side of her vehicle hit the other car, scraping up against the side, and that crash sent her vehicle careening back, back—

Toward Gunner's truck.

She turned her head. Saw him coming right toward her. Bright lights.

She braced for the impact.

"SYDNEY!" SLADE YELLED FRANTICALLY.

She wasn't talking to him now, but he could hear the scream of metal.

He spun around. Cale was running toward him.

"What's happening?" Cale demanded.

They were in the lobby of the EOD building. Mercer had finally finished grilling him. "I wanted to catch her before she left," he whispered. "I had to warn her—"

Cale grabbed his arms. "What's happening?"

"Sydney." The phone was still clutched in his fingers. "Her brakes stopped working. I could hear...I could hear her screaming."

Cale's eyes widened, and he whirled away. He started shouting orders, calling for a track on Sydney.

But it was too late.

Slade glanced down at his phone. The line had gone dead.

GUNNER SLAMMED ON his brakes. The scent of burned rubber filled his nostrils as he jumped from his truck. The accident he'd just seen had his heart thundering in his chest.

"Sydney!" He ran toward her. Moments before, he'd seen her frightened face in the glow of his headlights.

Her car had raced forward—then smashed into a light pole.

His shaking fingers curled around the door handle, and he yanked the door open. A cloud of white greeted him. The air bag. He shoved it back. "Baby?"

A groan slipped from her.

He started to breathe again.

"Gunner?"

Carefully, oh, so carefully, he unhooked her seat belt and eased her from the car. The other driver was out of his vehicle now. Yelling about fools who shouldn't be on the road.

Gunner lifted Sydney up against his chest. She felt small and fragile. Breakable. She seemed so fierce most of the time that he forgot just how vulnerable she could be.

He leveled a killing stare on the man who was yelling instead of checking to see if Sydney was hurt. The guy stopped midholler and backed up a few steps. "Call for help," Gunner snarled.

The guy nodded frantically and pulled out his phone.

Gunner carried Sydney away from the road. More cars had stopped now. Bystanders were trickling toward them.

He put her down on the nearby grass. Brushed back her hair. There wasn't enough light for him to see her face clearly. "Are you all right?"

She nodded. "The brakes didn't work," she whispered. "I couldn't stop."

Fear and fury battled within him. Another attempt on her life. This time, he'd been helpless.

"An ambulance is coming!" a voice called out. It sounded like the guy who'd been yelling minutes before.

Gunner slid his hands over Sydney's body, looking for any signs of injury. No broken bones. No cuts. But she winced when he touched her left shoulder. The seat belt would have cut into her there.

When he stopped his exam, she immediately wrapped her hands around her stomach. "I couldn't stop," she repeated again.

And he'd been helpless.

This ends now.

He pulled her against his chest and held her until he heard the wail of the ambulance.

When the EMTs rushed toward him, Gunner said, "She's pregnant. Just…please, make sure she's all right."

As she was settled into the ambulance, he finally looked around.

He saw that others had joined the crowd. Cale was there, with Slade.

Slade's haggard face told Gunner that he'd heard his words. The time for secrets was over.

"Meet me at the hospital," Gunner called out to Cale.

The other agent nodded.

Gunner wasn't letting that ambulance leave without him. He climbed inside and caught Sydney's hand.

"Gunner," Sydney whispered. "My stomach's cramping."

Tears stung his eyes. He held her hand tighter even as he bent and pressed a kiss to her lips. "It's going to be all right." The ambulance lurched forward, and Gunner began to pray.

SYDNEY WAS ON a special exam table. She was too early in her pregnancy for the doctor to hear the baby's heartbeat, so an emergency ultrasound had been ordered.

Gunner paced beside her, his expression even more fierce than normal.

The cramping had stopped, but the fear? Oh, yes, that was still there. She didn't want anything happening to the baby inside her.

Not my baby.

"Gunner, I'm scared." She could tell him. He was her best friend. Had been, even before they'd become lovers.

He stopped pacing and immediately came to her side. "Don't be. This baby is fine." His fingers twined with hers.

She wondered if he knew that she could see the fear in his gaze. Usually he was much better at masking his emotions.

Usually she was, too.

She stared down at her stomach, covered now by a green exam gown.

"I love you." Gunner's words were rough and rumbling, and at first, she thought she'd imagined them.

Because she'd wanted to hear them for so long.

Sydney shook her head, an instinctive move. He hadn't—

"I want you to marry me."

Now her gaze flew to his. "Gunner?"

His lips hitched up into a half smile. "This isn't the right place, is it? Not the right time. But I've never been *that* guy, Syd. The guy with the smooth lines and the perfect moves. I am the guy who loves you, though. The guy who'd give his life for you. Who'd do *anything* for you."

He wanted to marry her. Was this about the baby? Or—

"I want you. I love *you*." That half smile vanished. "Sometimes I think I started falling for you the first time I met you, but you were so far out of my reach then." He glanced down at their intertwined fingers. His hold tightened. "I still feel like you are. You deserve better than me, but I swear, if you give me the chance, I'll do everything I can to make you happy."

A knock sounded at the door; then, a few seconds later, a doctor and nurse were bustling inside.

The ultrasound technician was there, getting everything set up. She lowered Sydney's bed, angling it.

Sydney stared at Gunner. He was waiting for her answer.

Maybe Gunner had always been waiting, and she hadn't seen it. She'd noticed his silence, his watchful ways, but she hadn't realized what any of that meant.

Then she thought about their lives. The way he was always coming to her house in D.C. for dinner. The way he never forgot her birthday or the way he made sure that she never spent Christmas alone.

"Sydney?" Gunner asked.

"Yes," she told him, because if he wanted to build a future with her, she was more than ready to build one with him.

Gunner's face changed then. It lit up as she'd never seen it before. He didn't simply look dangerous or sexy just now…the man was gorgeous.

The monitor flickered on next to her. The ultrasound technician went to work. Sydney forced herself to concentrate on that monitor. She was afraid to look, but she had to do this.

"You're early on," the doctor said, "so what we're looking for is the sack…*well, well*…"

The doctor moved, blocking her view of the monitor. No, no, that couldn't be good. She squeezed Gunner's hand, probably cutting off his circulation.

But the doctor just smiled at her. "Some mild cramping early in pregnancy can be perfectly normal. The baby is fine." He nodded once, then said, "From the looks of things, they both are." Then he backed up and pointed to the screen.

As he moved his fingers and started talking, showing them the two tiny lives that were their babies, Sydney couldn't even hear his words. A dull roar had filled her ears.

Not one baby. Two?

She glanced back over at Gunner. She'd never seen a smile so wide.

And he'd asked to marry her, before he even knew about the baby's fate. He'd wanted *her*.

"Now, you're going to need to be careful. Carrying twins will mean that your body is doing twice the work."

Careful—not exactly part of life for the EOD.

"She'll stay safe," Gunner vowed, and she knew he meant the words.

Good, because she wasn't going to play the killer's game anymore. In that instant when she'd seen Gunner's headlights coming at her, she'd known that her chances for survival were running out.

No more games.

No more attacks.

The doctor finished up. Sydney dressed and Gunner went to stand guard outside her room. Even though she was afraid and had death stalking her, a bubble of happiness kept growing inside her.

Twins. Gunner. Marriage.

If she could just get the killer off her back, she'd have everything she'd ever wanted.

She pushed open the door.

"I'm sorry, Gunner, but you have to come with me."

Logan's words froze her.

"The hell I am!" Gunner snapped. He jerked away from Logan. "I'm not leaving Sydney's side. I'm not—"

"A witness saw you tampering with her brakes."

The words filled Sydney's ears.

She stilled. That bubble of happiness wasn't feeling so light anymore.

"And Sydney's neighbor had sent a lady out to house-sit while she and her husband were out of town. The house sitter *was* there that night, and she reported seeing your truck, just sitting out in the street, waiting, right before the fire started at Sydney's home."

Sydney shook her head. That bubble burst. "Gunner?"

He spun toward her. "It's *not* true. It's a setup!"

The nearby hospital staff started to ease back.

Sydney searched Gunner's face. Then looked at Logan. "Why are you doing this?"

"Because your life matters. I don't know what kind of game he's playing…" His jaw locked. "But it's ending."

Cale and Slade waited behind them, both watching with tense faces.

Sydney could only shake her head. "Gunner isn't the one playing this game. He's been saving me."

Slade stepped forward. "That's what he wanted you to think! He's not a hero. He never was."

Gunner's face seemed to have turned to stone.

"I won't believe this!" No, she wouldn't. "I trust Gunner." More than she trusted anyone else.

"Mercer wants him back at the office. *Now.*" Logan's voice was grim. "I'm sorry, but I have no choice here. Gunner's been termed a threat, and I have to take him in."

"Then I'm coming, too."

But Slade stepped in her path. "Why won't you see him for what he is? He's playing you."

Someone was playing her, all right.

"You can't have this much blind trust in him!" Slade's voice rose. "You're smarter than this!"

Yes, she was. The rest of the EOD should be, too.

She caught Logan's gaze. Read the message that her shock had almost blinded her to before.

Then she gave a quick nod. "I—I'm coming." But she let the faintest quiver slide into the words.

Gunner's eyes widened.

Slade's lips curved.

She realized that she'd just used the same quiver in her voice that Slade had used in his words a few times.

Maybe they were both good actors.

They were about to see who was better.

She wasn't letting Gunner go down for these attacks. No way.

"I think…I remembered hearing my captors talk about the *American*," Slade whispered as he rubbed his chin. "I told Cale on the way here."

He'd just remembered? Wasn't that convenient?

And bull.

"I think Gunner's been working with them all along, using his ties to the EOD to bring the drugs into the country."

"Enough." Logan's fierce voice. "We say nothing else until we're back in the office."

But Slade thought he'd said plenty. Enough to have her turning her back on Gunner?

The man didn't know her at all.

Only fair, since she'd just realized that she never knew him, either.

"SYDNEY CAN'T KEEP being in the line of fire." Gunner leveled his stare at Mercer. "She needs to be taken out of the equation *now*."

"Sydney's a woman with a very strong mind. Is that what she wants?" Mercer demanded.

Gunner flattened his hands on Mercer's desk and leaned toward him. "Sydney's not being risked anymore. Someone is using her to get at me." And he knew just who that person was.

Did Slade really think he was so smart? That no one saw through his lies?

Even being blood wasn't going to protect him.

"Haul his butt in here," Gunner demanded. "Lock him up. Keep him away from her." *And me. Before I tear him apart.*

"The house sitter did see you at Sydney's—"

"Really? Then where the hell was this person when the house was burning? Because no one came running out— no one tried to do a damn thing."

"She said she was scared. That she kept the doors bolted. She was just a kid, barely over sixteen." Mercer assessed him. "Why were you waiting outside Sydney's house?"

"Because I was getting up the damn courage to go and talk to her!"

Mercer raised a doubting eyebrow.

"And the witness who saw you tampering with her brakes?"

"I think the witness is already dead." Brutal, but true. "After he told you what he saw, he was dead. Because his words were a flat lie, and the real killer here isn't going to let him keep breathing."

Frowning now, Mercer reached for his phone. Gunner's teeth ground together as he listened to Mercer on the call. The big boss was demanding that the witness to the tampering be brought in, only...

Mercer glanced back at him. "He convulsed in holding, just a few moments ago. Tina's on scene. Says it looks like the guy overdosed."

"Get Tina to do the blood work," Gunner said as his mind whirled. "Because I'm betting you'll find *muerte* in his system."

Mercer gave the order, then hung up the phone.

"That's why he was making all those charter flights," Gunner muttered as he rose to his full height. "They were drug runs. He was making connections down there. Setting everything up." He raked a hand through his hair. "His accounts were cleaned out because he didn't plan on coming back to the U.S. He was leaving everyone—"

Leaving Sydney.

"Then he got into trouble down there." As if there wouldn't be enemies in the drug cartels. "He wanted us to bail him out." Only he and Sydney had almost died in the process.

Somehow Slade had survived. Thrived.

"He wasn't their captive." No, Gunner didn't think that had been the case at all.

The door opened behind him. A quick glance showed Logan coming into the room.

Logan, whose whisper-thin voice had ordered him to "Play along" at the hospital because he wasn't turning his back on him. The EOD stuck together.

Always.

"He was working us, the whole time. Slade wanted us down there so he could have an in at the EOD." So he could search their files. Make contacts to distribute the *muerte*. They'd thought he was an addict.

When he was the drug lord.

"Are you sure about all of this?" Logan shook his head. "We don't have proof, man. Every piece of evidence is pointing to you. We can't even bring in the FBI because they'd want to lock you up, not him."

"Because he's smarter than we realized. He's been working us all along."

"We need more evidence." Mercer stood behind his desk. "If Slade is behind the *muerte* spread, we have to bring him down and stop his whole cartel."

"Let him come at me," Gunner demanded. "Give him a straight shot at me. He hates me." That had to be obvious to them all. Otherwise, why plant all the evidence against him? "I can get you what you need."

But Mercer shook his head. "No, you can't." Definite. "You don't share with a man you hate. You share your secrets with those you love."

Sydney.

"He's tried to *kill* her," Gunner said, gritting his teeth. "I'm not risking her—"

"It's Sydney's life. She gets to decide the risk. Not anyone else."

"And she's carrying my babies," Gunner snapped right back. "So that means I get to—"

"Uh, babies?" Logan murmured, and coughed. "As in more than one?"

Gunner gave a grim nod.

"Hot damn," Logan said.

"So you see why I'm *not* risking the woman I love."

"You just—" Logan sputtered. "You just admitted to loving her? Who are you? Where's the real Gunner?"

Gunner ignored him. "She won't come in the line of fire. Use me. Set me up as bait, but not her. Not...*her*."

"I think that's my call." Sydney's voice. Sydney—pushing back a side door in Mercer's office.

Gunner shook his head. "Where the hell does that door even lead?" he muttered. Every time he'd been in there, that room had been blocked.

"In case any of our other staff members have been compromised," Mercer said as his gaze cut to Sydney, "I took the liberty of having Sydney come in the...uh...private entrance. I didn't want to advertise her presence with us."

He knew that Sydney had worked closely with Mercer on a few other cases. It appeared she was privy to more than a few of the man's secrets, too.

"You heard it all?" Mercer asked her.

Sydney nodded. Her gaze stayed on Gunner. "Slade isn't going to come clean with you."

"And he's been trying to kill you!" All while wearing that fake mask of concern. He'd been playing them from the first.

Gunner had known for sure when he spun around in the hospital and met his brother's gaze. The tragic concern there... Slade had worn that same expression at Sarah Bell's funeral. But an hour after the funeral, Gunner had caught the guy making out with another girl.

So much for his grief.

"Am I supposed to die, too?" Those had been Slade's

words, and the memory of them had stabbed into Gunner, sharp like a knife, as he stood in that hospital corridor.

"Slade didn't withdraw his application to the EOD," Sydney said.

Gunner shook his head, trying to banish that memory.

"I found his original file—"

"And I remember rejecting him," Mercer added, voice like a bear's growl. "I never forget men I think can be a threat."

Sydney moved closer to Gunner. "He was turned away from the EOD. I found his drug test. He didn't pass it then. He was on an unknown drug at the time, one that our labs couldn't identify, but it raised red flags."

"That's why we rejected him and stopped using him on freelance work," Mercer added.

Sydney's hand touched lightly against Gunner's arm. "I got Tina to compare his old drug test with the result that we had on the *muerte*...he was on *muerte* back then."

"Bring him in here," Gunner said, his heart feeling as if it were encased in ice. How had this happened? His brother. "We can show him the tests, make him talk—"

Mercer shook his head. "You don't think I've already run at him, again and again? This guy isn't going to break for me." Before Gunner could speak, Mercer added, "Or for you."

"That's where I come in." Sydney's smile was a little sad. "If he thinks that I believe him, if he thinks that I've lost faith in you, then he will come to me."

"More likely, he'll *kill* you!"

"Not with you, Cale and Logan watching my back." She seemed so calm. How did she seem so calm? He was about to go crazy. "I know you'll keep me safe." So certain.

"This won't work." He wasn't talking to the others. They didn't matter. Just her. "He'll kill you. He won't talk."

"He asked me to run away with him before that last trip to Peru two years ago. Before his plane crashed."

Gunner was too conscious of the pounding of his heart. Too loud.

"I didn't go with him because…things were getting difficult between us, so I told him that I needed more time. He told me that he wanted to offer me a brand-new life. One that I wouldn't be able to imagine." Her shoulders rolled. "He wanted to bring me into the new world that he was creating. Into the new *life* that he was starting for himself."

A life as a drug cartel leader?

"Do you know why they call the drug *muerte?*" Logan asked.

Gunner shook his head.

"I did some digging with a contact at the DEA. The drug is named after the guy who's spreading it through South America…a man who reportedly rose from the dead to take over one of the biggest cartels in Peru."

Slade. Rising from the dead…

"If Slade truly wanted to kill me," Sydney said, "all he had to do was walk up to me and put a bullet in my heart."

Gunner's hands fisted.

"Instead, he's been playing with me. Punishing me. Punishing you. Hell, maybe he's even been testing us, to see how far we'll go in order to survive." Her lips thinned. "I won't be tested again. Mercer is setting up my house in Baton Rouge. We're getting out of D.C. Making him think that I'm turning my back on you and on the EOD. Making him think that I only want—"

"—him," Gunner finished for her.

"And if I'm right on this, he'll come after me. He'll think we're alone, and I *will* get him to tell me the truth."

"Or what—die trying?"

Her hand lifted. Her fingers feathered over his cheek.

"That's where you come in, Gunner. It's your job to keep me alive. To keep all of us alive."

He couldn't get enough air into his lungs. "There's another way…."

"No, there isn't. I'm the only one who he might trust here. I'm the one who can get to him. I'm the one who can end this." Her hand dropped, and he immediately missed the warmth of her touch. "You can have me in your sights every moment," she whispered. "If you think I'm threatened, if you think I'm in danger—"

"Then I will *end* him."

Her breath expelled in a relieved rush. "Then you're in?"

"You aren't giving me a choice." He glared at them all. Promised Mercer and Logan all kinds of hell if this turned south. "And there's no way I'm letting you leave town without me."

She threw her arms around him and squeezed the breath right out of him. "I love you, Gunner." A whispered confession that he knew no one else heard.

But it was a confession that he'd never forget.

Chapter Eleven

Sydney had tears trekking down her cheeks as Gunner was loaded into the back of the black SUV. Men in suits were on either side of him. His hands were cuffed.

"Sydney?" Slade's voice.

She turned and saw him walking up, with Cale by his side. Slade's steps were slow as he approached her, the limp seeming to give him more trouble today.

She knew that Slade had been in the interrogation room. She'd been in hell.

It was easy to keep the tears coming. Maybe it was the hormones or maybe she'd always been a better actress than she'd thought. Either way... "Gunner's being taken in by the feds. They have so much evidence on him..." Her voice trailed away. "I thought I knew him."

Slade came to her and wrapped his arms around her.

She shoved him back. "Don't touch me!" Now, that part wasn't acting. "I can't stand— I can't trust anyone. I—I thought I could..."

Pain flashed across Slade's face. "You can trust me, sweetheart. You always could. I've never stopped loving you."

She blinked up at him, trying to get the tears off her lashes. "After what I did to you?"

What she'd done? *Nothing.* Lived her life, tried to help him.

He'd been lying to her for years.

"Always," he whispered as he lifted his hand and wiped away her tears.

She'd just told him not to touch her.

Her jaw ached, and she tried to ease the clenching of her teeth. "I have to get out of here." She let her gaze cut to Cale. She shuddered, and glanced back at Slade. "I need to get away, to think."

"Where will you go?" he whispered.

A sad smile curved her lips. "To the only home I have left."

Now he knew just where she'd be.

Would he follow her?

She turned away from him, but not before she caught the curling of his lips.

Yes, he'd follow.

Then come and get me.

SLADE WATCHED THE black SUV pull away from the curb, triumph filling him. His brother had been taken into custody. The agents had followed all the bread crumbs that he'd left behind, and everyone there had turned on Gunner.

His brother was alone.

Sydney was sliding into a cab now. She looked so pale. So lost. So...perfect.

"It is safe for her to be alone?" Slade asked, keeping his voice raspy. He'd also done a pretty good job of keeping up his limp, as if that injury really bothered him anymore.

Cale stepped to the edge of the sidewalk. "Now that we have Gunner, she'll be safe. She...she turned in her resignation when she found out the truth. Sydney doesn't want to be part of the EOD anymore."

The cab eased into the flow of traffic.

His Sydney. Going home.

He knew exactly where her home was. Since her place near EOD headquarters had been torched, she'd return to the only safe haven that she had—in Louisiana.

Now would be the perfect time to get to Sydney. She'd be alone, isolated in Baton Rouge as she hadn't been with Gunner dodging her steps in D.C.

Her guard would be lowered. No more EOD agents trailing underfoot.

Just Sydney.

Just me.

"This is where we say goodbye," Cale told him.

Slade turned toward him. "No more guard duty?"

"You were the one who was right all along. You'll be getting a full apology from the EOD, and compensation, of course."

Of course.

Cale offered his hand. "I wish things could have been different."

Slade took his hand. Shook it. "Maybe they will be now." Everything could be different.

He'd once planned to take Sydney away, to start a new life with her. Sure, he couldn't tell her about what he'd really done down in South America, but why should she ever have to learn that truth?

Maybe it would be the time for them to start fresh. To start over.

Cale walked away.

Slade began to whistle.

And if Sydney didn't want him…if she refused the offer that he made to her, then, while she was all alone in the swamps that she foolishly loved so much, he'd kill her.

Her mistake to leave all the protection around her. Sydney had always thought she was so smart and tough.

When, all along, he'd been the one pulling the puppet strings.

He walked down the sidewalk, still whistling and planning for his reunion in Baton Rouge.

THE HOUSE WAS too quiet. Sydney stood in her living room, far too aware of the silence that surrounded her. She was back in Baton Rouge, back in the house that she'd loved so much, for so long.

The place seemed to be filled with memories of Gunner.

She turned toward the large window in her den. If Slade showed up—*when,* not *if*—she was supposed to keep him in front of that window. Because this position would give Gunner a perfect shot at the other man.

Exhaling slowly, she looked out of that window. The edge of the swamp and twisting cypress trees stared back at her. She saw no sign of Gunner, but she could feel him.

Watching.

Protecting.

Cale was out there, as well. Stationed at another watch point and staring down his scope, too. They had the main windows under watch so that they could see into the house.

She'd taken care of making sure they could *hear* what was happening inside the house. A bit of surveillance equipment, carefully hidden, and they were linked into the audio feed. They'd hear anything that would be said tonight.

Logan would also *see* what went down, since he was in the surveillance van hidden in her garage, and he was watching every single thing that happened on the monitors in there.

Their intel had already told them that Slade had hopped a plane out of D.C. He was coming after her; it was just a matter of time.

Sydney kept staring out of that window.

When she'd first come home, she'd felt Gunner all around her. Remembered the way they'd made love in that house. She could even have sworn that the sheets in her room still carried his scent.

She'd seen the memory of him at the kitchen table—Gunner staring at her with his dark gaze, watching her so hungrily.

He was everywhere.

Did he understand how completely he fit into her life?

Headlights appeared in the darkness. Her heart beat a little faster.

Almost showtime.

Almost.

She put her hand on the glass. *I'll be safe, Gunner.*

Then she turned away.

GUNNER WATCHED SYDNEY put her hand on the glass pane. His own hand was curled around the weapon in his hand. He could see her lovely face so perfectly through the scope.

"Target is on scene," Logan said in his earpiece.

Just as they'd planned. So far, everything was going just according to Sydney and Mercer's plan.

They'd wanted to pull Slade out of D.C., to make him think that he was safe, that no eyes were on him.

Insects chirped around Gunner, and the swamp behind him stretched for miles.

The place was secluded, all right, and Slade would no doubt think it was the perfect spot for him to approach Sydney.

He'd be wrong.

But I still don't like this.

No way did he want Sydney alone in the room with his brother. Slade had become twisted, whether from the drugs or something else, and Gunner knew there were no limits to what the man might do.

Gunner wouldn't feel safe until Sydney was in his arms again.

"I have a visual." This came from Cale. "Target is leaving the vehicle and approaching the house."

Now they would see just what secrets Sydney would learn, and just how very far his brother had fallen.

"WE'RE OKAY," SYDNEY whispered as she belted her fluffy, terry-cloth robe. The robe was huge, but that was the point, right? To disguise what she was wearing underneath it.

A bulletproof vest.

Gunner had been adamant on that point. He wanted their babies protected. She did, too. She just had to make sure that Slade didn't see any sign of that vest.

The doorbell pealed. She glanced at the clock. Just a little after midnight. Her hand quickly ran through her hair, tousling it so that it would look as if she'd gotten out of bed. Then she waited a few moments, not wanting to rush to the door too quickly.

The doorbell pealed again.

With quick steps, she made her way to the door. She glanced through the peephole. Saw Slade's face under her porch light. Her hand flipped the lock and she opened the door. "Slade! What are you doing here?" Sydney thought she did a pretty good job of projecting surprise into her voice.

He smiled at her, the smile that had once made her think he was such a charming guy. The smile she now understood was a lie.

"I couldn't let you be all by yourself, sweetheart. Not when you were so broken up." He stepped over the threshold. She eased back, carefully putting distance between them. "You might think everyone has let you down, but I haven't."

Yes, you have.

He shut the door behind him, locked it. When he moved, she saw the slight bulge under his jacket. He'd come to comfort her, but he'd also brought a weapon?

He came to kill me.

Her breath felt cold in her lungs. She'd thought that he'd try to keep charming her first. Sydney hadn't believed that he'd go straight for the kill.

She backed up another few steps. He followed her, falling into line with her picture window. Perfect positioning.

"It's after midnight," she told him as she pretended to try to smooth her hair. "You shouldn't be here now."

"I needed to see you." His gaze raked over her robe. He frowned. "And you wanted to see me, or else you wouldn't have let me in the door."

Her head moved in a faint nod. "I needed to…I needed to talk with you. About Gunner. I didn't know that—"

"—he was a monster?" His gaze came back to her face. "Now you do. Now you know you were with the right brother in the beginning."

The right brother has you in his sights now.

She locked her jaw. "I didn't think that I could be so blind." She'd arranged things deliberately in the den. Her hand waved toward her computer. The screen was off now, but papers were scattered across the desk, making it look as if she'd been hard at work earlier in the night. "So I started digging on my own. The powers-that-be at the EOD might be satisfied with the way this scene played out, but I'm not."

Because she was looking so carefully for it, Sydney caught the faint hardening of Slade's eyes.

"The EOD did its job."

But Sydney shook her head. "I'm not sure of that. Gunner

was swearing to me that he was innocent, that he'd never hurt me, never do all of those things…"

"He's a liar, sweetheart." He stepped closer to her. Her gaze slid down to his legs, then rose.

She held her ground this time. She wanted to make sure they both stood in front of that window. With the lights on in the den, they would be shown perfectly. *Perfect targets.*

"I'm sorry, but you were wrong about him."

Another hard shake of her head. "I—I can't be wrong." Then she lifted her chin. "I went back, pulled all the records that I could find on the fire at Sarah Bell's house."

A long sigh broke from him. "Why put so much faith in him? You're only hurting yourself." His hand lifted. Trailed over her cheek. "Let me help you heal."

She hated his touch. "I found an old article online. Gunner's football team…they won the state championship that same weekend. The weekend of the fire at the Bell home."

His nostrils flared. "So?"

"So the state championship game was held in a city four hours away. Gunner was with his team the whole time. They went on a bus together. They came back on a bus together… He didn't start that fire."

His hand fell away.

She shoved her fingers into the heavy pockets on her robe. She had her own weapon stashed in one of those pockets.

"I did more checking," she whispered.

He spun away from her and paced toward the window. "On damn Gunner? Always…*Gunner.*"

"No. On you."

His shoulders stiffened. With it being just the two of them, he wasn't working nearly as hard to conceal his reactions. Maybe because he didn't care.

He'd also lost his limp.

"Sydney…" He sighed out her name. "I came down here to comfort you so we could be together again. I know you've always loved me."

"I did love you. Once." That feeling was nothing like what she felt for Gunner.

He was still staring out of the window, and presenting such a fine target. "Before Gunner," he growled.

"Before you started to change," she whispered back.

SLADE'S FACE FILLED Gunner's scope. The rage there, the hate, was frightening to see.

But Sydney wouldn't see it. She couldn't. Slade wasn't looking at her. He was just staring out into the darkness.

Planning his attack.

Gunner's left hand pressed against his transmitter. "He's going to make a move soon. Be ready." That much fury couldn't be held in check for long.

They were wired into the audio feed that Sydney had set up, so they were hearing every word that she said. She was baiting Slade, pushing him.

That pushing was working.

Gunner hadn't been at a state championship game the weekend that Sarah Bell died. The game had been two weekends after the fire. But it looked as though Slade didn't remember that.

A flaw in his plan.

Then Sydney started talking again, and Gunner felt sweat trickle down the side of his face.

"YOU MADE SO many trips down to South America before— before—"

"Before Gunner left me for dead?" He turned toward her, his face expressionless. "Let's not forget that part. Gunner and *you* both left me."

"I wondered about all of those charter trips. Especially when I discovered that every account you had was empty. Cleaned out."

His lips curved. The sight was chilling.

"You'd become angry before that last trip, too. I remember the fights we had. You accused me—"

"—of cheating?" he finished. He glanced down at his hands. Both hands had fisted. "I thought you might be sleeping with Gunner back then. I saw the way he looked at you, and the way you looked at him."

"I wasn't—"

"Not then. But now?" His eyebrows climbed. "You're going to try telling me that the baby you're carrying isn't his?"

"It is." *They* are. "And that's why I had to keep digging. I couldn't give up on him. *I couldn't.*"

"You should have." So soft.

She kept talking. "It was when I was digging, trying to find where all your money went to...that was when I discovered that you'd set up extra accounts in the Caymans."

He laughed. "You and your damn computers. You could always find out too much on them." He reached into his jacket and pulled out his weapon. "Like I said, you *should* have stopped."

GUNNER'S FINGER TIGHTENED around the trigger.

"Hold!" This was Logan's order, growled through the transmitter. "She's still got him talking. We need to learn as much as we can."

They needed to make sure that not a single bullet so much as grazed her skin.

"Hold, Gunner. That's a direct order."

He wasn't following orders now. He was protecting the woman he loved.

Slade hadn't aimed the gun at her yet. It was still by his side. The second that gun started to rise…

Gunner would fire. Brother or no brother.

"I FOUND OUT you were never the man I thought you were. Even before your plane went down…back then, you were drug running, weren't you?"

He laughed, and completely dropped the mask that he'd been wearing. The twisted fury and hate was there for her to see, burning so hot. "Yeah, I was. I was earning more money than I'd ever made in my life. Those jerks at the EOD had turned me away. Said I was too unstable. Screw that! I was the best they could've had, and they wouldn't even give me a chance."

Her hand tightened around the weapon that was still concealed in her oversize robe pocket. "So you took your own chance?"

"I took the jobs that came to me. I made connections… money…so much money." He rolled his shoulders. "You don't know what it's like to have nothing. *I do.* I grew up with nothing. Dirt-poor on a reservation in the middle of nowhere. No father. No mother. I wasn't even raised by my blood. The grandfather that Gunner talks about so much? *Not mine.*"

"But he took you in," Sydney said. "He helped—"

"My father signed custody of me over to him. Said I'd be with *family.* I didn't want to be with them. I didn't want Gunner's castoffs. Didn't want to always be in his shadow."

There was pain there, breaking through the fury.

"I swore I'd do anything I had to do in order to get out of that place. I wouldn't be poor again. No one would look down on me." His smile flashed—not the charming one, But the cold grin of a killer. "Do you have any idea how much money I have? How much power?"

"No…" *Tell me.*

"I am *muerte.* I found it on one of my runs. I knew I could take over down there. When you and Gunner came for me the first time—"

When they'd all nearly died.

"I was fighting for power then. Your entrance, your backup…it was appreciated." The grin kept chilling her. "Of course, it would have helped more if you hadn't abandoned me."

"You were dead!"

"Actually, yes, I was."

Her breath burned in her lungs as surprise rolled through her.

"But thanks to the *muerte,* I came back."

"I don't understand."

"My men dragged a doctor to me—some relief worker they found. He brought me back, I don't even know how… injections, luck. Hell, maybe the devil just didn't want me. The doc even said that the *muerte* might have saved me, that it was working in my body, stopping the blood loss."

"What happened to the doctor?"

"When I recovered, I slit his throat."

Brutal. But she knew that was exactly who—what— Slade was. A brutal killer. "And you became the cartel ruler down there?"

"I am *muerte.*"

"Why?" She breathed out the word as if she was frightened. And she was. The man before her was a walking nightmare. "Why did you want the EOD to come and rescue you? You were free and clear. We thought you were dead. Why—"

"Because I was ready to expand. I knew that you'd taken out Guerrero recently…."

The Mexican arms dealer. Now everything was connecting. Her heart thudded into her chest. "He had links to the drug trade. That's why you accessed his file at the EOD, you wanted to know—"

"I wanted to know what assets of his I could still use in Mexico, and what assets I needed to eliminate."

"You mean kill."

"Yes." A shrug. "I knew it would be easy enough to get that intel from inside the EOD."

"So you worked us all…you threatened Hal—"

Another cold laugh. "I paid him. There was no threat. Of course, I never intended for him to live long enough to collect his cash."

"And the shooter? The man who fired at me—"

"I connected with him while in rehab." The gun was held loosely in his hand at his side. She was tense, her gaze drifting to the gun far too often, but he acted as if he wasn't even aware he'd pulled out the weapon. "You can meet the most useful contacts in the oddest places."

"You hooked the guy up with *muerte*."

"In return, he agreed to take a shot at you. I *did* tell him to miss, by the way. That was just a scare shot."

"And at my house? The fire—"

His smile vanished. "I was supposed to be the one to save you."

"Were you supposed to save Sarah, too?" Whispered.

"No, I wanted her to burn."

She had never known him at *all*. "What about when we were in Peru—that shot on the beach? That was you, wasn't it?"

"Guilty."

How had he gotten the gun then? Had he arranged for one of his men to meet him?

"Figured it was never too early…to start driving a wedge between you and Gunner." He glanced down at the weapon.

His sigh seemed a little sad. "Now, I'm afraid, you are going to have to die."

She shook her head. "Slade, no, don't do this!"

"But I don't have a choice. As soon as I heard what you had to say…that you'd found evidence, your fate was set." He was still staring at the gun. "You won't stay quiet, and I can't take the chance of you ruining things for me. I've got big plans. I'll use the assets of Guerrero's that will work for me. I'll bring my trade right up the border…I'll have so much money and power that no one will ever be able to touch me." His gaze came back to her. "But you have to die first."

He was going to do it.

She backed away, easing toward the couch so that she could drop and have some sort of cover. "You still have a chance," she told him. "Don't—"

"You're the only one who knows the truth about me."

He watched her with the unflinching gaze of a snake, ready to strike.

Sydney shook her head. "No." Then she dropped her own mask. Let the fear slide away and let her own fury burst free. "The EOD knows, too. Logan, Cale and Gunner? They've been listening to every single word that you said. And guess what? You're in their sights now."

Eyes widening in shock, he swung back toward the window. Sydney dived behind the couch.

"No!" Slade screamed.

"Yes," Gunner whispered.

Slade whirled from the window and lifted his gun toward the couch.

Gunner's finger squeezed the trigger. The bullet flew through the window, shattering the glass, and slammed into Slade.

One shot.

The man staggered, then tried to aim again.

Gunner fired once more.

Even as that second bullet found its target, Gunner saw Logan burst into the den. Logan raced toward Slade as the man slumped to the floor.

Over.

Because he'd just put two bullets into his own brother.

"CLEAR!" LOGAN YELLED.

Sydney rose from behind the couch. Slade was on the floor, with Logan over him. There was blood, a lot of it, and she hurried toward the men.

Slade's eyes were open. He was glaring up at Logan, even as Logan held his gaze and his gun right on the other man. "You're being taken in," Logan told him. "We've got your confession recorded. You're not getting away."

Slade clenched his teeth. "I…I'm not going in! I won't—"

"You don't have a choice," Logan growled. Then he talked into his transmitter. "We need that ambulance. Send the EMTs through." He leaned over Slade. "The wounds aren't fatal. You'll stand trial for what you've done. *Muerte* won't survive—"

"You think…I'll…roll on the cartels? They'd *kill* me…"

The front door flew open. Sydney glanced up. Gunner was there, racing toward her.

He grabbed her in his arms and held her tight. She could feel the thunder of his heartbeat against her chest. "You're making me lose too many years of my life," he muttered.

Not anymore. The nightmare was over. He was clear. Slade was contained. It was *over.*

An ambulance's siren roared outside.

"The big hero…" Slade groaned. "You think this…is how you stop…me?"

Gunner lifted his head but didn't ease his hold on Sydney. "You're my brother." He shook his head. "How the hell did you wind up like this? I was there for you when we were growing up, keeping you safe, making sure—"

"Sure that I was in your shadow." Slade heaved up. Blood pulsed from his wounds. "No...more."

Gunner's body was as hard as a rock against hers. She could only imagine the pain that he had to feel. His own brother had been setting him up, willing to let Gunner spend his life in jail.

The siren kept wailing outside. The EMTs had been kept close, as a precaution, and in moments, they were rushing inside her house.

Logan eased back a step so that they could get to their patient. Logan had already taken Slade's gun and bagged it for evidence.

But when the EMT reached for Slade, Slade's body started convulsing. His eyes rolled back in his head. He jerked and twisted. The EMT swore and leaned over him.

That was the moment when Slade yanked out the backup weapon from the holster on his ankle. He moved so fast—so very fast—and had that weapon at the EMT's head in seconds.

Everyone froze.

Everyone...except Slade and his hostage.

Even as the blood darkened his shirt, he rose to his feet. Slade yanked the young EMT up, keeping the man in front of him. "Drop your guns," Slade ordered, "or I will put a bullet into his head right now."

Gunner stepped in front of Sydney, shielding her with his body. He didn't drop his weapon.

"Drop it, *hero*," Slade snarled. "Or watch him die."

"P-please..." the man begged.

She couldn't see his face, but she could hear his fear. The tension in the room weighed down on them all. She heard the shuffle of footsteps. Slade and his hostage, backing up a bit.

Backing up…and that retreat would put them right in front of her broken picture window.

Was Cale still positioned on the other side of the house? Or had he moved? She hadn't been hooked in to their transmissions, and she didn't know if he'd been repositioned when Gunner rushed inside.

Her palms were sweating, her heart racing too fast.

"I'm not going to…jail…" Slade said. "And sorry, brother, but you're not getting…the girl…."

Her hands grabbed for Gunner because she knew Slade was about to take the shot. "No!" Sydney screamed.

The blast of gunfire shook the room.

But Gunner didn't fall.

"Syd…ney…"

Slade's voice.

Gunner rushed forward, and she saw that Slade had been hit again, only this time, this time she knew the wound was fatal. Slade's skin was ashen, his eyes barely staying open. The EMT had lurched away from him, and Gunner had caught his brother's body just as Slade fell.

Sydney glanced toward the window. Another bullet hole had broken the glass.

Cale.

Protecting his team.

"Slade?"

She glanced back at Gunner's voice. He was curled over Slade's body holding his brother's hand.

Slade seemed to be trying to stare up at him.

Two brothers.

"Can we…go in the woods…?" Slade's voice. Weak with pain, sounding lost. "I want to go…with you…Gun…"

She saw Gunner's throat move as he swallowed.

"Is…Grandpa comin'?"

Slade didn't sound like a man anymore. More like a lost child. Maybe in those last moments, he was.

"Grandfather's already waiting for you," Gunner said, his own voice rumbling. "Go on to the woods. Stay with him. I'll join you later."

"P-promise…?" Slade's breath rushed out. His chest stilled.

Gunner's hand clenched around his. "I promise."

Sydney wrapped her arms around Gunner and held him as tightly as she could.

THE GRAVE WOULDN'T be empty this time. Gunner stood, silent, during the service as his brother was put to rest. Sydney was by his side, her small hand cradled in his. Logan was on his right. The friend who'd never doubted him. The friend who'd always be there.

Jasper Adams had come to the service, too. The ex-EOD agent waited across from Gunner. Jasper's wife, Veronica—Cale's sister—had her arm curled around his waist.

And Cale…he watched the proceedings just as silently as Gunner.

When Gunner had taken his shots, he'd tried to keep his brother alive.

When Cale had fired, there had been no choice. To save Gunner, he'd had to take the kill shot.

But Cale still looked at him with guilt in his eyes. He shouldn't do that. Gunner would have to talk to him soon, have to make the other man realize—

I understand.

The service ended. The small group walked away, all but Gunner and Sydney. They lingered for a moment. He looked at the flowers. Thought about his brother. "I want to remember him the way he was, back when we were kids."

Going for hikes in the woods.

Once, Slade had loved those hikes as much as Gunner had.

Once.

"Then remember him that way," Sydney whispered. "Remember him happy. Remember the good parts."

He glanced over at her. Sweet Sydney. His saving grace.

"Remember the love, and push everything else away."

He bent toward her and rested his forehead against hers. "I love you." He'd told her before, but he needed to say the words again. He wanted to say them, over and over.

Her soft hand slid over his jaw. "And I love you."

A gift. One he'd always treasure, just the way he treasured her.

His head lifted. He cast one last look toward his brother's casket.

Remember the love. Push everything else away.

"Enjoy your walk in the woods, brother. One day, maybe I'll see you again."

Until then, he'd be walking with Sydney. With the children they had on the way. He'd remember the love, he'd show those children so much love...

And with Sydney, he knew they'd be happy. He'd prove that he could be a good father. A father his children would be proud to have.

They turned away from the grave. The sunlight was so bright. It chased away the shadows, and it showed him the hope that waited. With Sydney. With his friends.

With the life that would be. All he had to do was just reach out and take that life. Just reach out…

He turned Sydney in his arms, held tight to her and kissed her.

And he knew he'd found his perfect home.

Epilogue

Getting called into the big boss's office couldn't be a good thing. Cale squared his shoulders and swung open the door that would take him into Mercer's inner sanctum.

Mercer glanced up, no expression on his face, and waved Cale toward him. "Have a seat."

Right. Nodding quickly, Cale took the offered seat.

Mercer's fingers drummed on his desk. "It seems that you're working out quite well as a member of the Shadow Agents."

"Sir, they're a good team." Good people. But taking that shot, taking out Gunner's brother...that shot was going to haunt him.

Every death did.

"And you're a good asset to that team. Cool under fire, determined and willing to do whatever's necessary for the mission."

Cale stiffened. He didn't like that "whatever's necessary" part.

"So I think you're going to be the perfect man for a very special assignment."

Cale leaned forward.

"It's an assignment that has the *highest* priority at the EOD." Intensity deepened Mercer's voice. "I want a man on this case, a guy I can trust one hundred percent." He stopped drumming his fingers and pointed at Cale. "Are you that man?"

"Yes, sir."

"You'd better be," Mercer muttered. "Son, you'd damn well better be...because if you fail on this mission, if *anything* goes wrong, I will make you regret it the rest of your life."

Cale managed to keep his expression neutral, with a whole lot of effort.

"Are we clear?"

Cale nodded.

"Good." Mercer flashed a smile that Cale was sure had made plenty of men shudder in fear. "Then get your bags packed, because you're going to Rio."

The door closed behind Cale Lane. An interesting man. A dangerous man.

A man who'd better be the right choice for this mission.

Mercer opened his drawer. Carefully he pulled out the file for this case. He flipped through the dossiers, then paused when he saw her picture.

Cale had *better* be the right choice.

Because if this mission went wrong, if *anything* happened to his daughter...

"I will make you regret it the rest of your life." Cale had no idea just what hell he'd bring down on him.

Because Mercer never made threats.

Just promises.

* * * * *

COMING NEXT MONTH from Harlequin® Intrigue®
AVAILABLE AUGUST 20, 2013

#1443 BRIDAL ARMOR
Colby Agency: The Specialists
Debra Webb
Thomas Casey's extreme black ops team is the best at recovering the worst situations. When thrust into the most dangerous situation of his career, can he recover his heart?

#1444 TASK FORCE BRIDE
The Precinct: Task Force
Julie Miller
A tough K-9 cop masquerades as the fiancé of a shy bridal-shop owner in order to protect her from the terrifying criminal who's hot on her trail.

#1445 GLITTER AND GUNFIRE
Shadow Agents
Cynthia Eden
Cale Lane is used to life-or-death battles. But when the former army ranger's new mission is to simply watch over gorgeous socialite Cassidy Sherridan, he follows orders.

#1446 BODYGUARD UNDER FIRE
Covert Cowboys, Inc.
Elle James
Recruited to join an elite undercover group, former army Special Forces soldier Chuck Bolton returns to Texas. And his first assignment is to protect his former fiancé...and the child he's never met.

#1447 THE BETRAYED
Mystere Parish: Family Inheritance
Jana DeLeon
Danae LeBeau thought she'd find answers when she returned to her childhood home, but someone doesn't like the questions she's asking. And the guy next door will stop at nothing to find out why.

#1448 MOST ELIGIBLE SPY
HQ: Texas
Dana Marton
After being betrayed by her own brother, can Molly Rogers trust an unknown soldier to save her and her son from ruthless smugglers who are out for blood?

You can find more information on upcoming Harlequin®
titles, free excerpts and more at www.Harlequin.com.

REQUEST YOUR FREE BOOKS!
2 FREE NOVELS PLUS 2 FREE GIFTS!

HARLEQUIN®

INTRIGUE®

BREATHTAKING ROMANTIC SUSPENSE

YES! Please send me 2 FREE Harlequin Intrigue® novels and my 2 FREE gifts (gifts are worth about $10). After receiving them, if I don't wish to receive any more books, I can return the shipping statement marked "cancel." If I don't cancel, I will receive 6 brand-new novels every month and be billed just $4.74 per book in the U.S. or $5.24 per book in Canada. That's a savings of at least 14% off the cover price! It's quite a bargain! Shipping and handling is just 50¢ per book in the U.S. and 75¢ per book in Canada.* I understand that accepting the 2 free books and gifts places me under no obligation to buy anything. I can always return a shipment and cancel at any time. Even if I never buy another book, the two free books and gifts are mine to keep forever.

182/382 HDN F42N

Name	(PLEASE PRINT)
Address	Apt. #
City	State/Prov.	Zip/Postal Code

Signature (if under 18, a parent or guardian must sign)

Mail to the Harlequin® Reader Service:
IN U.S.A.: P.O. Box 1867, Buffalo, NY 14240-1867
IN CANADA: P.O. Box 609, Fort Erie, Ontario L2A 5X3
**Are you a subscriber to Harlequin Intrigue books
and want to receive the larger-print edition?
Call 1-800-873-8635 or visit www.ReaderService.com.**

* Terms and prices subject to change without notice. Prices do not include applicable taxes. Sales tax applicable in N.Y. Canadian residents will be charged applicable taxes. Offer not valid in Quebec. This offer is limited to one order per household. Not valid for current subscribers to Harlequin Intrigue books. All orders subject to credit approval. Credit or debit balances in a customer's account(s) may be offset by any other outstanding balance owed by or to the customer. Please allow 4 to 6 weeks for delivery. Offer available while quantities last.

Your Privacy—The Harlequin® Reader Service is committed to protecting your privacy. Our Privacy Policy is available online at www.ReaderService.com or upon request from the Harlequin Reader Service.

We make a portion of our mailing list available to reputable third parties that offer products we believe may interest you. If you prefer that we not exchange your name with third parties, or if you wish to clarify or modify your communication preferences, please visit us at www.ReaderService.com/consumerschoice or write to us at Harlequin Reader Service Preference Service, P.O. Box 9062, Buffalo, NY 14269. Include your complete name and address.

HI13R

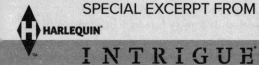
Read on for a sneak-peek of USA TODAY *bestselling author
Debra Webb's first installment of her brand-new*
COLBY AGENCY: THE SPECIALISTS *series,*

Bridal Armor

*At the airport in Denver, Colby Agency spy Thomas Casey
is intercepted by the only woman who ever made him
think twice about his unflinching determination to
remain unattached...*

She flashed an overly bright smile and handed him a passport. "That's you, right?"

He opened it and, startled, gazed up at her. "Who are you?"

"You know me," she murmured, leaning closer. "Thomas."

His eyes went wide as he recognized her voice under the disguise.

"I need you." The words were out, full of more truth than she cared to admit regarding their past, present and, quite possibly, their immediate future.

He nodded once, all business, and fell in beside her as she headed toward an employee access. She refused to look back, though she could feel Grant closing in as the door locked behind them.

"This way."

"Tell me what's going on, Jo."

She ignored the ripple of awareness that followed his using her given name. It wasn't the reaction she'd expected. Thomas always treated everyone with efficient professionalism. Except for that one notable, extremely personal, incident years ago.

"I'll tell you everything just as soon as we're out of here." She checked her watch. They had less than five minutes before the cabbie she'd paid to wait left in search of another fare. "Keep up. We have to get out of the area before the roads are closed." She'd taken precautions, given herself options, but no one could prepare for a freak blizzard.

"Are you in trouble?"

"Yes." On one too many levels, she realized. But it was too late to back out now. If she didn't follow through, someone more objective would take over the investigation. Based on what she'd seen, she didn't think that was a good idea.

Moving forward, she hoped some deep-seated instinct would kick in, making him curious enough to cooperate with her.

"Jo, wait."

Would the day ever come when his voice didn't create that shiver of anticipation? "No time."

"I need an explanation."

"And I'll give you one when we're away from the airport."

Can Jo be trusted or is it a trap?
Then again, nothing is too dangerous for these agents...
except falling in love.

Don't miss
Bridal Armor
by Debra Webb
Book one in the
COLBY AGENCY: THE SPECIALISTS SERIES

Available August 20, edge-of-your-seat romance,
only from Harlequin® Intrigue®!

Copyright © 2012 Debra Webb

HIEXP0913

SADDLE UP AND READ 'EM!

Looking for another great Western read? Check out these September reads from the SUSPENSE category!

COWBOY REDEMPTION by Elle James
Covert Cowboys
Harlequin Intrigue

MOST ELIGIBLE SPY by Dana Marton
HQ: Texas
Harlequin Intrigue

*Look for these great Western reads and more
available wherever books are sold or visit*
www.Harlequin.com/Westerns

SUART0913SUSP

HARLEQUIN®

INTRIGUE®

*HE WAS ASSIGNED TO PROTECT HER...
NOT MAKE HER HIS OWN.*

Cale Lane had his orders: keep Cassidy Sherridan alive at all costs. But who sent six armed men storming the Rio ballroom to take her out? The gorgeous party girl wasn't giving it up. Now he had a more urgent mission: uncover Cassidy's secrets...one by one.

GLITTER AND GUNFIRE

BY *USA TODAY* BESTSELLING AUTHOR

CYNTHIA EDEN

PART OF THE SHADOW AGENTS SERIES.

*Catch the thrill August 20,
only from Harlequin® Intrigue®.*

HI69712